HAZARDOUS UNIONS

Two Tales of a Civil War Christmas

Alison Bruce & Kat Flannery

HAZARDOUS UNIONS

Alison Bruce: www.alisonbruce.ca

Kat Flannery: http://www.katflannery-author.com

FIRST EDITION TRADE PAPERBACK

Imajin Books —www.imajinbooks.com

September 7, 2013

ISBN: 978-1-927792-32-2

Cover designed by Ryan Doan —www.ryandoan.com

Praise for Hazardous Unions

"Maggie and Matty Becker will enchant you as they struggle for respect, survival, and love in the Civil War's troubled time. You'll sigh with pleasure as you finish each story." —Caroline Clemmons, author of *Bluebonnet Bride*

"Two very talented authors, Alison Bruce and Kat Flannery, teamed up to write *Hazardous Unions; Two Tales of a Civil War Christmas*. It is the story of twin sisters, Matty and Maggie Becker who are separated at the beginning of the Civil War....One major thing ties them to each other— their upbringing by loving and wise parents. As their stories unfold, they are both able to make a difference in the lives of the people they hold dear. They each solve a different mystery and, at the same time, fall in love. They also witness a form of racism within each of the families, reflecting the mores of the north and the south. The characters and the times are well depicted in this short novel. I highly recommend this novel to Civil War enthusiasts and readers who enjoy a well-written historical romance. If you like intrigue, mystery and romance, this book is for you. It will hold your attention and is a quick read that you won't be able to put down." —Katherine Boyer, Tear a Page Blog

"Double your reading pleasure with twin passions—two novellas featuring twins Maggie and Matty, and heroes who'll steal your heart. Alison Bruce and Kat Flannery penned stories that play on your senses like a sonata. A must read!" —Jacquie Rogers, award-winning author of *Much Ado About Madams*

"*Hazardous Unions* are twin stories about the adventures of two sisters during the Civil War and the dilemmas they get themselves into. Maggie's story, written by Alison Bruce, tells the tale of a Northern young woman who accepts a job as housekeeper to a Southern family...A wonderfully entertaining and well written novella, with engaging characters and appropriate language for the era. Ms. Bruce knows her history. I will be eager to read more of her work. Matty, by Kat Flannery, is equally delightful. Unlike her sister, Matty stays in the North working for a Union General...Even in the midst of war and danger and death, love will have its way, as it does with Maggie and Matty." —Charlene Raddon, author of *To Have and to Hold*

Dedications & Acknowledgements

All that we see or seem is but a dream within a dream.
~ Edgar Allan Poe

I'd like to thank Alison Bruce for agreeing to partner with me on this book. You are a plethora of talent and I am thrilled to have had the opportunity to work alongside you.

HAZARDOUS UNIONS wouldn't have been possible without the help of Cheryl Tardif, my publisher, for your guidance, kindness, and encouragement. My Editor, Todd Barselow for sharpening my words to perfection, you're amazing. Tammy Ivanochko for reading everything I hand her, and offering great advice. Thank you from the bottom of my heart.

Many thanks to my readers for your continued support; I could not do this without you.

Love,
Kat

This book is dedicated with love to my uncle, Dennis George. He said write romance and I did, with humor.

A big thank you goes to Kat Flannery who invited me to partner with her on a historical romance. It was an honor to be asked—even if it did lead to months of research. Speaking of which, I must thank my fellow authors who share their knowledge of American history via Cowboy Kisses and Western Historical Romance Book Club.

To my good friends and beta readers, Nancy O'Neill and Melodie Campbell, my editor Todd Barselow, and my publisher Cheryl Tardif, thank you for your patience and good advice. And big hugs to my children, Kate and Sam, who made sure dinner got made and dishes washed when I was writing.

Alison

MAGGIE

By Alison Bruce

Spring 1861

Dearest Matty,

I miss you more than I would ever have thought possible.

When we set out, I felt I was on a grand adventure. Then we reached St. Louis. The city has changed since we were there together, travelling west with Mama and Papa. It isn't so much the landmarks that are different, though the city has grown. It is the climate. All around me I could feel a level of excitement about the coming war that was almost frightening. No one doubts that war is coming, but truly, sister mine, I wish they had read their history. What they are wishing upon themselves is not the glorious venture they all expect.

We stayed in St Louis a few days, waiting for Captain Hamilton's daughter to arrive. You might remember me mentioning that she has been attending Wheaton Seminary, in Massachusetts. I was curious to meet her. I do not imagine many southern aristocrats send their daughters to northern schools. I learned that Mrs. Hamilton suggested this course for her stepdaughter and it is a cause for tension between them. Patience Hamilton, who could not have been less aptly named, greeted her father with touching warmth and her stepmother with an icy chill.

The Captain, that is the Major, for he has already been promoted since joining the Confederate Army, paid for the best accommodations for our trip down river. Since I was the only female servant in their entourage, Madame insisted that I share a cabin with Patience. Another source of tension I wish I could have avoided. Despite this, the voyage was pleasant.

We now continue overland to Bellevue, the Hamilton home plantation. I will send this letter back with the river boat, however. I do not expect I will be able to send a letter to you again until the war is over.

I have been told that Bellevue is lovely, but as Mama would say, "Lovely is as lovely does." Already I have seen some of the evils of slavery described in Mrs. Beecher-Stowe's novel. I fear I will see worse before long.

As the Bible says, and Papa often quoted, "I am a stranger in a strange land."

Your loving sister,
Maggie

CHAPTER ONE

Fall 1862.

The Yankees were coming.

We'd seen the signs days ago. News was, most of west Tennessee had fallen under Union control. Thaddeus scouted them out while hunting rabbits in the brush that bordered the plantation's cotton fields. We'd prepared as best we could as fast as we could, and now I was waiting for them on the front veranda of Bellevue.

"Why me?"

"Someone has to meet them, Miss Maggie," Mammy said, setting out tea things as if the neighbours were coming to call. "Mrs. Hamilton hasn't got your nerve and Miss Patience wouldn't be a lick of good even if she would come downstairs."

"I'm just a servant," I objected half-heartedly.

"Yeah, like Tad here is just a dumb nigger." Mammy cocked her head to one side and a moment later I heard the faint but shrill whistle of the kettle. She smoothed the skirt of her greying white pinny over her faded grey dress. Eventually, the two garments were going to match. "Watch out for her, boy," she said, before heading around the corner of the wraparound porch toward the kitchen door.

Only Mammy could get away with calling Thaddeus "boy" or "nigger" without coming under the resolute stare of a man who looked like he could have been carved out of a huge block of obsidian. Mammy was his aunt and had raised him, along with Major Hamilton, from nursery age. The boys had been more like brothers than master and slave, Mammy said, until Master Ned was sent off to West Point to be made an officer and a gentleman. It was hard for me to reconcile her picture of

Master Ned with the aloof man who had employed me to take care of his wife.

I was barely sixteen when I was hired by the Captain, now Major Hamilton. Some days I felt that I was twice that age now, instead of just a couple of years older. Today, watching the Union contingent approach, I felt like that frightened girl again. I took small comfort in the pair of pistols hidden in the pockets of my crinoline. Knowing that Thaddeus was watching over me from the shadows, armed to the teeth, was more reassuring.

Half a dozen hard looking men approached the house. Four of them spread out, some facing us, some partly turned to keep an eye on the out buildings. Two of them rode up the path towards the porch. I felt like I was being ringed in by a pack of hungry wolves. The leader of the pack rode up to the bottom of the front steps.

Wolfish was a description that fit him. Hard muscled, wary eyes, shaggy dark hair spiking out from his cap, he looked old with experience and young in years. His uniform had seen better days and his beard was untrimmed, but it appeared that he had made some effort to clean up before approaching the house. That was a good sign.

I had also made an effort for appearances sake. Instead of my usual long braid, I had twisted my blonde hair into knot and allowed tendrils to fall free on either side of my face. I was wearing one of the calico dresses Mrs. Hamilton bought me in St. Louis. She wanted to make it clear that I was no mere servant any more. I was using it today for similar reasons.

"Afternoon, ma'am. I'm Captain Seth Stone. I have a cavalry troop under my command that needs to set up quarters for the winter."

"I see." My voice was steady, but I could feel my knees wobble beneath my skirts. "And?"

"And this looks like a good place to stay."

"How many are you expecting us to accommodate?"

I heard a chuckle from one of his men. It was stifled with a sharp look from the grim-faced sergeant behind the captain.

"Not so many as there should be," the Captain said, ignoring the interruption. "If you'd oblige me by asking your man to lay down his arms, maybe we can discuss terms."

"*Gott hilf mir*," I prayed, but held my ground. "You have your protectors, Captain. I have mine."

With a hand gesture, he signaled his men and they all dismounted as neatly as if they were on parade. Then he dismounted and held out his reins to the sergeant.

"Thaddeus, would you lead these troopers and their horses to water?"

Thaddeus stepped out of the shadows, empty handed. "Yes, miss."

The two men passed on the stairs. Thaddeus was significantly taller and broader than the Union officer and was doing his best guard dog imitation. The Captain didn't flinch when they passed. He did keep his eye on Thaddeus until he was in the range of his own men. Then he turned his attention back to me and I lifted my head up to make eye-contact. He may not have been as tall as Thaddeus, but he was not a small man and I am on the short side for a woman.

Having asserted his dominance, he backed up a step.

"I understand this is the Hamilton home. Are you Mrs. Hamilton?"

"No, sir. I am Magrethe Becker, Mrs. Hamilton's companion."

His eyes widened. "Maybe I should be speaking to the lady of the house."

"Mrs. Hamilton is indisposed and asked me to..." I stopped, looking for the right word. Meet with him? That sounded too friendly. Deal with him? Almost rude. "Negotiate terms with you."

He let out a short bark of laughter.

"My terms are simple, Miss Becker. I need to winter seventy men and three officers, plus myself. It'll be tight, but this place looks like it has enough room with the house and out buildings. We'll need food and fodder of course. You can either offer, or I will take."

I shook my head. "No."

He barked out a longer laugh. "What makes you think you're in the position to say no?"

"Twelve wounded union soldiers in our care, Captain Stone."

For a moment his expression gave me a rush of fear. I half expected him to growl.

"I want to see them."

"Of course. But let us finish talking terms first."

His hand went to his sidearm. I took a step back.

"Miss Maggie?"

I nearly jumped out of my skin. I had been so intent on the Captain, I hadn't heard the front door open. Labelle, Mammy's kitchen helper, was trying to hide behind the tea trolley while pushing it out onto the veranda.

"Yes, Labelle?"

"Mammy thought you might want some mint tea, Miss Maggie," the young woman said, nodding her head so hard she was going to give herself a headache. "And there's some of Mammy's biscuits and honey."

"Could you ask Mammy to send some biscuits down to the stables? I imagine the Captain's men are hungry."

"Already done, Miss Maggie."

Labelle ran back into the house, leaving me to pour tea. I gestured toward the wicker chair and the table set out with cloth, plates and cups.

Captain Stone removed his hat and, like the gentleman he was by act of Congress, waited for me to sit.

"Bellevue has been serving as an ad hoc hospital since the battle at Shiloh. We've had more than a hundred wounded men come through here," I explained as I served. "Mostly they were Confederates, but they brought us wounded Union prisoners as well. When we knew that the Federals were taking over the area, we convinced the Confederate commander that it would be better for everyone to leave the wounded Union soldiers here." I handed the Captain his tea.

"As insurance."

I swallowed my anger with a sip of tea before speaking. "Some of them wouldn't have survived moving or prison life. Some of them still might die but we have been doing our best for them. And you are welcome, sir."

"I meant no offense."

"No?" I shook my head. Anger was better than fear, but I could ill afford to give into either. Instead, I directed the conversation to logistics. "We have space for your officers in the house and the barns are mostly empty. The Confederates took most of our livestock and all our horses."

"I saw a row of six cabins when I rode in."

"They house the plantation workers and their families. You can ask them to help you set up camp, but I won't let you displace them."

The Captain leaned forward in the wicker chair, his free hand gripping the armrest. I suddenly realized the brilliance of Mammy's tactics. A man holding a delicate teacup is at a disadvantage.

He stared at me for a minute or so then stated, "You won't let me."

Resisting the urge to look away, I sipped my tea and pretended to be calmer than I felt. He didn't look so big and rough close up, but that stare reminded me of Thaddeus, who in turn reminded me of my father. Papa had a stare that could bring the most cocksure young man into line. An excellent skill for a teacher or a cavalry captain.

"President Lincoln is making free men of the slaves. Would you turn a freeman and his family from his home without just cause?"

He leaned back, the hard look replaced by an expression of amused confusion.

"You don't sound like any southerner I've ever met."

"I'm not a southerner. I was born in New York and moved to Kansas with my family. After our father died, my sister and I went to work for officer's wives at Fort Leavenworth to help my mother and younger brother. I stayed with the family I was placed with, and here I am."

"Working for the southern aristocracy on a cotton plantation."

"No offence, Captain, but while your words say north, your accent says south."

I mentally reviewed officers I had met in the Hamilton household and dismissed Tennessee, Kentucky and Virginia as possible home states. His accent put him deeper into the south, making him as out of place in the Union cavalry as I was on a cotton plantation.

"I have a few men who were well enough to stay with the company but could use some nursing. I want them put up in the house as well as my officers. Other than that, we will abide by your terms so long as my men are well fed and have a roof over their heads."

I nodded. "Your men will be as well fed as anyone can be in these times. If your men can hunt, that will be helpful as we have no hogs or cattle to slaughter and the chickens are needed for laying. With careful management, we may have enough flour and sugar to last the winter."

"If we get the supply lines going, we might be able to supplement the dry goods."

I nodded again. "That would be most helpful."

"Then we have a deal, Miss Becker?" he asked, standing and offering me his hand.

We shook on it.

"What business does she have making a deal with a damned Yankee?" Patience demanded. "We're at war with those hypocritical scoundrels."

I had discovered that Miss Patience had learned to question the institution of slavery while at school, but parroted her father's views on the inviolate right of each state to decide its own destiny.

Mrs. Hamilton tried to soothe her stepdaughter, but Patience turned away with an impatient huff. At times such as these, I wanted to slap both of them.

"That's enough, Miss Patience," Mammy said. "Miss Maggie did the best she could for us, better than anyone could have hoped for."

Spinning around to face Mammy, Patience balled her fist in anger. "You forget your place, Mammy. I'm not your nurseling anymore."

"Then stop acting like you are"

We were gathered in the attic nursery. It was the one place in the house that was secure from intrusion. I had been using it since I arrived at Bellevue. Patience moved up when she gave her room to be used for the hospital. Mrs. Hamilton had moved down to use old Mr. Hamilton's bedroom on the ground floor, but the Captain commandeered that room and library as his quarters.

Mammy had had a room off the nursery since she'd been brought inside to act as wet nurse to Master Ned. Thaddeus had turned a corner of the lumber room, which occupied the rest of the attic, into his quarters when the Major brought him back to the plantation. There was nothing odd about all of us being up here together, so it had become our headquarters.

"What is the real problem, Miss Patience?" Thaddeus asked. "This isn't just pride."

"My home taken from me. My life turned upside-down." Patience pressed her hands together as if in prayer. "What do I have left but my pride? Maggie could have resisted. She could have made a show of caring what happened to Bellevue. But she has no pride, no sense of place. She doesn't care about what happens to us. She's put us all at risk."

I gave my head a little shake. I agreed I had no real pride in Bellevue, but I cared about the people here. While Mrs. Hamilton cajoled and Mammy scolded, I saw what Thaddeus was getting at.

"Who don't I care about?" I asked. "Who have I put at risk?"

My questions produced an awkward silence.

"You didn't," Mammy said. "Tell me you weren't that foolish, Missy."

"He wouldn't leave," Patience said.

"Lord have mercy," Mammy groaned, looking heavenward.

Thaddeus' gaze was in the opposite direction and I almost muttered an unladylike "Oh, hell."

"What are you talking about?" Mrs. Hamilton asked. She turned to each of us in turn, looking for answers. She finally found it in her stepdaughter's flushed face.

"Oh, hell."

When the wounded started pouring toward Bellevue, my estimation of Miss Patience rose immeasurably. The young lady I had come to see as a spoiled brat at once put aside her pride and prejudices, rolled up her sleeves and dug into the work at hand. It turned out that she had a natural affinity for nursing. She hated the surgery and despised the surgeon that turned the dining room into an abattoir, but she was a wonder at following his directions to the cleaning and changing of bandages. She was seemingly tireless in serving the living and easing the dying.

In contrast, I gathered up the organizational reins that had been dropped by Mrs. Hamilton who had withdrawn to her room since hearing the news from Shiloh. I gained the respect of the household, but in truth, I would have rather done anything than the heartbreaking work Patience excelled in. She truly lived up to her name.

Probably every young man she nursed fell in love with her, and not just because of her heart-shaped face, lustrous brown hair and perfect figure. Only one had that affection returned. The younger son of a neighbour, Nathaniel Wentworth, was beneath Miss Hamilton's notice before the war. Now he was a war hero. Fortunate enough to be sewn up instead of sawn up, he stayed with us as long as he did because he contracted a fever. Now, it seemed, he was still with us.

Mammy put the kettle on. Tea was scarce, but mint and chamomile grew like weeds around here. She had other herbs she'd brew up as well, but tonight she was making chamomile mint tea. Chamomile to calm the nerves. Peppermint to clear our heads.

"Now that you've established that Nate is a romantic fool," Patience said, sounding more like her old self, "can we figure out what to do to keep him safe? He cannot be left out there with nothing more than a bedroll."

"Of course not, my dear," Mrs. Hamilton said. "Though in fairness, Patience, that is how he was faring for the past year or more. On patrol, your father and his men often had little more."

"My father was hale and hearty then. Nate is still recovering from his wounds."

"He should go home," I said. "Wentworth Place is smaller than Bellevue. The Union Army might have left it alone. We need to find out."

"That's a sensible suggestion," Mrs. Hamilton said, a gratifying but ill-timed comment. Anything Mrs. Hamilton agreed with was automatically disagreed with by Patience.

"And how do you propose we do that? Go down and ask? 'Oh, Mister Captain, sir, can you tell us which of our neighbors are likewise occupied by your forces?'"

I smiled. "Good idea. I'll do that tomorrow morning. In the meantime, do you think you could bring Lieutenant Wentworth in out of the cold, Thaddeus? I'm thinking he could spend the night with our people."

Patience objected, of course. "Put him with the slaves? He won't do it."

"He'll do it if I asked him to," Thaddeus. "I can be very persuasive."

"Thank you," I interjected before Patience could speak. "Now we can rest assured that the Lieutenant will be safe tonight."

Later, when I said my nightly prayers, I thanked God for keeping us safe so far. "Please keep Matty and Mama and Werner safe, wherever they are. And Papa, if you're listening, give me the strength to get through tomorrow without killing Patience."

CHAPTER TWO

Frost decorated the windows, diffusing the predawn light. I would have appreciated it more if I could have stayed in bed. Instead, I washed in icy water and dressed as quickly as I could. Then I redressed, picking a gown that was less faded and more flattering to my figure, which could be best described as sturdy. Good German stock.

Usually I headed down the back stairs, straight to the kitchen where I knew I could warm up. This morning I took the main stairs and did a quick inspection en route. Soldiers had been in and out the house throughout the evening. From the look of things, none seemed to appreciate that they were making use of someone's home. Fortunately, the rugs had been taken up and the portable valuables had long since been packed away.

"We'll need extra help in the house," I announced, walking into the kitchen. "And more lye soap."

Labelle already had the stove and ovens fired up, water boiling and stew cooking. She looked up from the pot she was stirring. "I can ask Mama Lou if she can spare a few more girls. But she's short-handed with the work those horse soldiers are creating. Might be better if *you* asked, Mammy."

Mammy was rolling biscuits, her specialty. She looked over to the two girls peeling potatoes and a third coring apples. They'd spend their day peeling one vegetable or fruit or another when they weren't washing something. That was before soldiers descended on us. Now they might be asked to do anything from turning a spit to turning a patient.

Fresh loaves of bread and a slab of bacon had been brought up from nearby brick building that combined bakery, smokehouse and quarters for the house slaves and Mama Lou.

"I could have a chat with Mama Lou," Mammy said, "but if *you* was to ask her first, Miss Maggie, she'd be a mite quicker to help. Then we could work out the details later."

"While complaining to each other that I have no idea how much field work still needs to be done."

Mammy grinned. "Exactly."

To think I once thought that slaves were bound to obey every order, immediately, without question. Of course, they obeyed. If they disobeyed they could be whipped or worse. But if you wanted a job done well, you needed to know who and how to ask. This was especially true now.

"I'll do it. After I make coffee."

"I should hope so, Miss Maggie."

About an hour later, I had a mixture of roasted acorns and dandelion roots brewing on the stove. In another pot, raw acorns were soaking. By tomorrow they'd be peeled and ready to roast. Patience declared it was foul stuff and once said I was trying to poison her. Mrs. Hamilton politely declined in favor of tea. Mammy, Thaddeus and I needed our morning coffee and put up with my poor imitation. I was betting that Captain Stone's men would feel the same. Speaking of whom...

"You have coffee, Miss Becker?"

Captain Stone was disheveled and looking worse for wear. I hoped he was feeling the effects of last night's carousing.

"Something like coffee. I'll have a pot ready soon if you want to try it."

His nose wrinkled at the bitter smell. "Thank you. I think. That isn't what I came to speak to you about, however. Your watchdog was out late last night. He was almost shot by one of our sentries."

"Thaddeus?"

"I believe so. He said he was hunting."

"That would explain the brace of rabbits hanging in the larder," I said, turning back to the stove.

"Twilight and daybreak are the usual times for hunting, not the middle of the night."

"That's probably what the rabbits think, too. In any case, Thaddeus doesn't hunt rabbits. He traps them and then breaks their necks. If he left them out all night, other predators might get them."

"Regardless, please tell your boy not to go out after dark without clearing it with me first."

I slammed the pot down on the stove top. The cast iron responded with a dull clang and a splash of water from the pot sizzled on the hot surface. Across the room, Labelle drop a pan she had been drying. Mammy scolded the girl for being clumsy.

"Thaddeus is a free man, manumitted by Major Hamilton many years ago," I said, brandishing the coffee pot as I turned to face the Captain. "He is employed by the family, just as I am. And, I might add, if he is a boy, you are a babe in arms."

His eyes widened. "Excuse me?"

Mammy chuckled. "Don't worry none, Captain. If Miss Maggie was a bit sharp with you, it's just 'cause she needs her coffee. Her brew tastes pretty good, but it just ain't the same."

There was some truth to Mammy's statement, but it irritated me nonetheless. Thaddeus was a good servant without having a servile bone in his body. That's how I liked to see myself. Perhaps that's why I took attacks upon his independence personally, especially from an officer that was probably fresh out of West Point at the start of the war.

Thinking of what Mama would have said about my manners and the folly of losing my temper, I pushed down my anger. "How sharper than a serpent's tooth it is to have a thankless child," my father might have quoted. Or perhaps Matty would have said it for him. Both were addicted to poetry.

"My apologies, Captain. Mammy's right, I shouldn't have been so sharp. Will you try a cup?" I waved the pot and he backed up a step. "It's not coffee, but it's not poison either."

I poured us each a cup without waiting for his answer. While he sniffed the brew, I poured cups for Mammy and Labelle.

"I'd like to discuss arrangements with you, if I may," I said. I sat at the table and invited him to do the same. He did, but he still hadn't tried my brew. "I assume that the men staying in the house will be eating here, too. We'll have breakfast ready for them soon. How do you want to organize the feeding of the rest of your men? Do you have cooks? Our families usually cook for themselves, but we do have a cookhouse for preparing meals for the field hands."

"We have cooks and equipment in our supply train, which should be with us later today. I'll have my quartermaster discuss the arrangements with you."

"Of course." I'd lived at Fort Leavenworth long enough to get an idea that the commander didn't take care of details like that, but it was an opening. "Your quarter master might also want to negotiate with our neighbors for extra supplies. Bellevue is mostly given over to cotton, but smaller plantations like Wentworth Place and La Fontaine are more diversified." Well, so were we, now, but I didn't need to mention that.

"Most of the local homes are hosting troops, including Wentworth and La Fontaine. You'll forgive me if I don't give you particulars."

I blushed. "I'm not a spy. I just want to make sure no one goes hungry."

His lips twitched, and I got the impression he was silently laughing at me. So be it. I had the information I needed. Lieutenant Wentworth couldn't go home. What in heaven's name were we going to do with him?

I took a gulp of ersatz coffee and made a face. Not my best effort. Next time I'd add some chicory root.

"It's not that bad," he said, after taking a sip. "It could use a little sugar."

I pushed the bowl toward him.

"There is something else, Miss Becker." He helped himself to a generous amount of sugar. "There will be times when I'll need to meet with my fellow officers, including our regiment commander. This house is large enough and centrally located, so we may meet here."

"And?"

"And, at those times I will insist on tighter security."

"If you are thinking of Thaddeus or me for that matter, you have nothing to worry about. We are loyal to the Hamilton family, but we are not Confederates."

"I suppose it's easier for dependents to walk that line. Supporting the Confederate cause was required by my family and when I could not..." His voice trailed off and he stared off at a point over my shoulder as though seeing the past there.

"I can't speak for everyone, Captain, but I think you will find that Tennessee is a border state in more ways than geography. The plantation owners may support the south, the rest of us are less concerned with politics than keeping body and soul together. However, I think you will find that people will be more sympathetic to your men if you get them to wipe their feet and use the ashtrays and spittoons instead of the floor."

I had the pleasure of seeing the Captain blush. Now I just had to make sure Lieutenant Wentworth didn't undo my work.

It was late morning before I was able to visit Mama Lou. By that time I had a plan.

Mama Lou was the matriarch of the field and farm slaves. Labelle told me her mother had come with the Major's first wife from New Orleans. When Madame Hamilton died, Mama Lou left the house, never to set foot inside again. She never lost her Creole accent, though most of her life had been spent at Bellevue. I loved listening to her, but sometimes she gave me the collywobbles. Like Mammy and Thaddeus, she wasn't the least bit servile. Unlike them, she showed evidence of her disobedience and there were times I wondered if she would have murdered all slave holders in their beds if she could have got away with it. Major Hamilton's solution was to put her in charge of the slave quarters. There were also times when I wondered if she would have happily murdered her charges there, too.

"*Bonjour cheri.*"

"*Bonjour* Mama. *Comment allez vous?*" One of the reasons that Mama Lou liked me was that I spoke a little French. Papa had been fluent in French, English and Latin as well as his native German. Our brother Werner was the better student, but Matty and I could get by in French and German.

"*Pas trés bien.* These soldiers are worse than the rebs for being horn dogs. How am I going to keep my girls safe? And what am I supposed to do with that *cochon* Tad has given me?"

"We need more help at the house. Send me the most vulnerable girls and Mammy will keep them safe and busy."

"And how will I get everything done?"

"Captain Stone says his supply train is due soon. They'll have people to put to work. We just have to find a way to make the Yankees think it's their idea."

"You think, *cheri*?"

"I hope. I'm working on the principle that cooperation will get us more than confrontation. I only hope I can keep us safe without crossing the line."

She laughed. "I heard from *ma fille* how well you were doing with that." She patted me on the hand. "You keep it up, *cheri*. Whatever you are doing is working so far. Now what about that *cochon*?"

"I have an idea, but I'll need some help."

Mama Lou provided me with a basket of herbs, salve and bandages and I headed for the slave quarters. I was ready to explain, if stopped, no matter what they might have heard, some families took care of their slaves when they were sick or injured. No one stopped me.

In fact, the only family member likely to go into the slave quarters was old Mr. Hamilton and that wouldn't have been to see to the sick. He was gone now and, heaven forgive me, I could not be sorry. A more lecherous old man I have never met. Thanks to him and his ilk, there were several mulattos on the plantation.

Thaddeus met me in the hut where Lieutenant Wentworth was being kept. It was a bachelor house, with only a few men left living there and they were in the fields. The lieutenant was alone, in a corner, sitting on the floor with his back to the wall.

Other than his boots and cap, he was out of uniform. What was left of his natty officer's greys had been cut off him during surgery, and burned shortly after. By going through her father's and grandfather's old clothes, Patience had managed to outfit her beau. The result was ill-fitting, ill-matched and perfect for our purposes.

When he saw me, he struggled to his feet. "Where is Miss Hamilton? Why are you keeping me here? Please say that you are here to take me somewhere more suitable."

"I could take you to the cavalry captain, sir. Miss Patience wouldn't be pleased, but if that's what you want."

He rubbed his eyes. "I shouldn't have stayed behind. I'll sneak away at nightfall."

He could have saved me great effort if he'd thought of that earlier.

"No," I sighed. "Tempting as that is, I can't let you."

His expression reminded me of Captain Stone's when I said no to him.

I felt Thaddeus at my shoulder. Wentworth got the message because his lips pressed into a tight line, holding back any remarks he might be tempted to make. Since I needed his cooperation, I tried to appeal to his romantic feelings.

"Don't you think Miss Patience has gone through enough this past year without you adding to her troubles? Her grandfather died last winter. Her father was captured by the Union in the summer. Her home was turned into a hospital where she was reunited with old friends only to comfort them while they died. Of the young men she grew up around, you are the only one she knows is alive and well."

Even in the shadows, I could see him grow pale. I pressed my point.

"The only good thing to come out of those weeks of trial was discovering her love for you. I will not let you break her heart by getting yourself killed. Not here. Not now."

"Why? She doesn't even like you," he said.

"I don't like her much either, or you. I'm still going to try to help the two of you."

"Why?"

"Damned if I know." I clamped a hand over my mouth and I could feel my cheeks redden.

That made him laugh. "Tell me how you're going to help me, Miss Maggie."

"We're going to hide you in plain sight," Thaddeus said, as I gathered my wits. "If you'll take a seat, sir."

I'd watched Mama trim Werner's hair often enough that I felt comfortable taking the scissors to the lieutenant's head. In any case, the result didn't have to be stylish, just short. Most field slaves kept their heads shorn to keep down the lice and ticks. When I saw how his hair curled, I left enough hair to cover his head with a woolly cap.

Fortunately his hair was almost black. His eyes were brown and a year of campaigning had tanned his skin. A little walnut oil mixed with goose grease darkened his face, hands and forearms a shade.

"I just want to say that I think this is a bad idea. I'm no minstrel performer. No one is going to believe I'm a nigger."

I bit my lower lip to keep my mouth shut. I'd already shamed my Mama with one unladylike retort today.

"Keep your head down and your mouth shut," Thaddeus advised. "Isn't that what a good nigger does?"

I switched to my upper lip, this time trying not to laugh.

"Not bad except for the nose," Thaddeus said.

"Too Roman," I agreed.

Wentworth huffed. "It's called 'patrician' and it's a family trait."

"Wrong family," Thaddeus said. "The Hamiltons have broader noses."

Wentworth looked blank, then it dawned on him what we were implying. Under his tan and brown stain, he flushed a deep red.

"It's either that or we say that your father strayed into the Hamilton... uh..." I floundered. I knew for a fact that such things happened, but I couldn't say it. I'd said enough, however.

"I thought you were a lady."

POP! Thaddeus jabbed Wentworth in the nose. The lieutenant was knocked back and would have fallen if the wall hadn't stopped him. One hand gripped the wall to keep him from sliding down. The other covered his face.

"Sit down, Lieutenant," I said, voice hardly shaking at all. "I'll give you something to stop the bleeding. I think the nose problem is solved."

I tried to twist a piece of cotton rag into a plug but my hands weren't cooperative. Wentworth took care of the task himself. By the time he was done, I had packed my basket and composed myself.

"You are correct, I am no lady. I am a housekeeper. As Lieutenant Nathaniel Wentworth, I am beneath your notice. As Nate, a mulatto field worker, you will take orders from me. Tomorrow morning, when the bell rings, you will join the work crew that Thaddeus is overseeing for the day. When the noon bell rings, you'll stop for dinner, then you'll go back to work again until the evening bell calls you in from the field. You will, as Thaddeus advised, keep your head down and your mouth shut. If you don't like it, run away if you dare."

Thaddeus followed me out of the cabin. He walked a half-step behind me, for appearances, but close enough we could converse comfortably.

"Do you think he'll run?" I asked.

"No. Mind, he might flee if he ever finds out you came to me earlier and asked me to break his nose."

"And if Patience finds out, *I'll* have to do the running."

I would have been glad of a cup of tea and a little time to myself when I got back to the kitchen. Tea was made, but it was part of a lunch tray for Mrs. and Miss Hamilton. Since everyone else was busy preparing food for the soldiers, it was up to me to carry it up. The tray was too wide for the backstairs so I shouldered open the door that led into the dining room and almost crashed into Captain Stone.

"I've been looking for you, Miss Becker."

I put the tray on the sideboard. "You found me," I said mopping up spilt milk. "How can I be of service?"

"Your people are being less cooperative than I hoped."

"Oh? May I suggest you give me a little more than a half day to set things in motion?"

I gave him a polite smile and picked up the tray, which he took from my hands.

"Where are you taking this?"

"Up to Mrs. Hamilton and her stepdaughter."

"Allow me. On the way you can tell me what you are setting in motion."

I explained that there was a chain of command on a plantation just as there was in the army. One layer in the hierarchy had been removed when the last of the white overseers had been drafted by the Confederates and circumstances had shifted the chain a little, but there was still an order to things.

"So, you have your sergeants, just as I do," Stone said.

"I suppose. In a way." I stopped. We had reached the bottom of the attic stairs and I didn't want to take this conversation within earshot of the Hamiltons. For that matter, I didn't want to take Captain Stone within range of the Hamiltons either. "It's more like I know who the sergeants are and how to negotiate with them. I don't have any real authority here, but since Major Hamilton was captured, I've taken on additional responsibilities."

Stone's brows creased in puzzlement. "Didn't Hamilton appoint a steward?"

"His father was still alive and in charge when the major left Bellevue. We've had word that he was captured, but we don't know if he received the letter telling him his father died."

"I'll see if I can get a message to him."

"Thank you. Perhaps you could enclose a message from Mrs. Hamilton. She was able to keep things running until she learned of his capture. Since then, she has barely left her rooms."

"And Miss Hamilton?"

"Miss Hamilton is not suited to household management. Fortunately she is well suited to nursing because I assure you I am not."

"I meant, would she like to include a message to her father?"

"Oh. Yes. Very probably. I'll ask her." I took the tray from him. "Thank you for your help, but I should take it from here. Mrs. Hamilton may not be presentable for visitors."

He gave me a shallow bow and there was a smirk on his face when he straightened.

"You're laughing at me," I said. "Why?"

"You say you have no real authority."

"It's true."

He gave a snort of laughter and left me.

I climbed the stairs, wondering what the captain found so funny.

Now, if Matty were here, she'd see the real humor in the situation. She was the one who told me I needed to stand up for myself. She didn't want me to stay with the Hamiltons, told me I was too easily put upon, but Mama said it wouldn't be for long. "Mr. Lincoln will get things settled in a trice," she said. "Mrs. Hamilton needs you, Maggie, and she's been good to you."

Mama was right. Compared to Matty, I had an easy employer who was generous and kind. Mrs. Hamilton made sure I was respectably clothed, well-fed and adequately rested. She even allowed me to practice on her beloved pianoforte, a square instrument that she'd carried with her from post to post since marrying the major. She had to leave it behind at Fort Leavenworth. Given that sacrifice, I didn't have the heart to desert her.

"Is that you Maggie?"

I pushed open the door at the top of the stairs. "Yes, ma'am. Sorry I'm late. Captain Stone waylaid me."

I was surprised to see Patience sitting with her stepmother. Despite what I told the captain, she usually had her midday meal later. Partly this was because she helped her patients with their meals. Mostly, she avoided me and her stepmother whenever possible. Normally, I would share the noon meal with Mrs. Hamilton. I served Miss Patience my portion.

"Is everything all right with Nathaniel?"

Of course, I thought. I should have known. "Everything is fine."

"I think Patience would like a little more detail than that," Mrs. Hamilton said. "Please sit down Maggie and tell us what has been arranged."

I found myself an extra cup and poured myself some tea before starting. Patience glared at me, but I was not going to do any more talking without some refreshment. I took a sip, then gave them the short version of my visit to Lieutenant Wentworth, without mention of the broken nose, of course.

"I don't like it, of course, but it is a solution," Mrs. Hamilton said. "It grieves me to say it, but my father-in-law's habits do make the deception plausible. I am only thankful that your father, Patience, did not share your grandfather's vices."

Patience focused her attention on the slice of egg pie on her plate. Unlike his son, Mr. Hamilton had not remarried when his wife died. No doubt, Patience saw this as loyalty to her grandmother whereas I suspected he preferred a free reign for his lechery.

I changed the topic. "Captain Stone has offered to send a message from you to Major Hamilton." Silence. Did they not understand my words? "He's going to make sure the major is well for you."

"I don't believe it," Patience said. "It's a trick."

"I don't see how," I said. "Or why. What does he have to gain? The only thing we can offer is our cooperation and so far he has that."

Patience gave a very unladylike snort. "You are cooperating. I am not a collaborator."

"Enough, Patience!" It was the first time I had ever heard Mrs. Hamilton raise her voice to her stepdaughter. "We have no choice whether Captain Stone and his men stay or go. Do not fool yourself by thinking otherwise. Instead, let us get something out of this unfortunate situation. If Captain Stone can ensure your father is alive and well, I am willing to accept his services."

Patience pressed her lips tightly together. I think she was as surprised as I was at Mrs. Hamilton's vehemence.

"I will write a letter this afternoon," Mrs. Hamilton said, sounding her usual calm self again. "Will you write your father, Patience?"

"To have my words used against him?"

"I don't think that corresponding with your father would count as collaboration," I said. "It may even bolster his spirits and give him strength to stand up to his enemy. Of course, it would have to be cleverly worded to get past the censors." I was adapting a trick I had learned from Papa. He used it when his students, including Matty and myself, complained his assignments were too difficult.

While the ladies ate in thoughtful silence, I left to make Mrs. Hamilton's bed and tidy her room. When I returned, I saw my employer looking upset and wondered what Patience had done now.

"We have discussed the situation and decided that Nathaniel should be brought up to the house," Patience said. "We could use the extra help and it would be far more appropriate to field work."

"No." Both Hamilton women stared at me as if I just sprouted horns. I softened my tone. "You will agree with me when you think it through, Miss Patience. You would be risking his life. The masquerade is good enough if he stays with the other workers, but bringing him into the house would draw attention to him. Also, what if one of the Union patients recognizes him? He might be taken for a spy."

Mrs. Hamilton's gently nodding head showed me that she understood. "It makes sense, Patience."

"Of course you'd take her part."

"It's not just the danger," I said, before Patience could start bullying her stepmother again. "Think of his pride. He has to act the part of a slave, which is bad enough for any man." Slaves included, I thought. "But to ask him to do that in front of the woman he cares for..." I let the thought hang in the air.

It was too much to expect Patience to agree with me, but she gave me a curt nod. For the sake of her peaceful digestion, I retreated to the kitchen. Perhaps, if I was lucky, Mammy would have something left for me to eat.

CHAPTER THREE

I got three days of relative peace before the next crisis.

"Miss Becker, are you sprinkling sugar under the table?"

It wasn't a surprise to see Captain Stone in the kitchen. He managed to find time to come in for cup of coffee at least once a day. The question was a bit odd though.

"Excuse me, Captain?"

"I know you have the room cleaned daily but by lunch, the place is crawling with ants again. And the flies! You wouldn't think there'd be so many flies in November."

"It isn't sugar that is attracting the ants and flies. It's blood."

He poured himself a cup of coffee and topped up my cup before sitting across from me. "They used the dining room as a surgery? Please tell me we're not eating off the table they used."

"They didn't use the table for surgery. It was moved to the parlor and used as a makeshift bed. For surgery they use a couple of pine boards between two sawhorses. We had basins on hand and a tub for the severed limbs, but the surgeon wasn't very careful where things landed. I imagine buckets of blood have seeped through the floor boards by now."

"Good God!"

"We did our best to clean up afterward, but blood doesn't go away easily. Evidently, it's more usual to use upper rooms for surgeries, in which case we might have had blood soaking though the ceiling. I'm not sure if it would be better or worse."

He stared at me. Since he did this regularly when we spoke, I had already noted that his eyes were grey-green, except when he was very tired. Then they were just grey. Today they were mostly green, which was also going to be the shade of his complexion if this conversation continued.

"When you say 'we' you don't mean that you assisted in the surgery, do you?"

"That depends on what you mean by assisted," I said with a shrug. "I am not a surgeon or a nurse. I cleaned surgical instruments, made sure there was a steady supply of hot water for washing and coffee to keep us all alert. We ran through our entire supply in a matter of days."

His eyes widened in surprise. I was used to seeing this, too. His response had been similar when I told him about the raids on our family's farm by the Missouri Militia. For a military man, he seemed to shock easily.

"Our supply of coffee," I explained. "Our supply of bandages and lint too, but those were easier to restock from the linen closet."

"You did all that?"

"Not by myself."

I also made sure that the surgical waste was burned, not buried. Papa's history lessons had taught me that in war, death by disease was as common as death by wounds. With help from Mammy, I found willing and able women to help Patience with the nursing, and strong-backed men to act as orderlies or dig graves. There were many tasks like that which fell to me to organize because the surgeon was too tired and Mrs. Hamilton had taken to her bed.

As if he heard my thought, he asked where Mrs. Hamilton and Miss Patience had been during the crisis.

"Miss Patience was nursing the wounded survivors. Mrs. Hamilton was ill, but she directed us to give what aid we could while making as few demands as possible on the household."

"I see."

"We all did our best," I insisted, sensing his scepticism.

"I understand."

If he understood, why did he look so irritated? I tried a more practical tact. "Borax helps keep the pests down. If you could get us more, we could spread it in the bad areas. I imagine there are a fair number of ants in the parlor as well."

He nodded. "Anything else?"

"Besides coffee, tea and sugar? Any supplies you could get would probably be welcome. Iodine. I am sure Miss Patience could use more iodine. She tells me it is essential for keeping wounds from becoming infected."

Again the captain nodded. "Borax. Iodine."

There was something else bothering him. I hoped it wasn't anything I'd have to lie about. "Lies have short legs," my mother told us when she caught us fibbing. Captain Stone struck me as the type who would catch a lie quickly. It was probably a standard part of officer training. In any case, I didn't want to lie to him if I could help it.

"About Miss Patience," he said eventually.

I schooled myself to wait for the question and not dive into trouble by anticipating it.

"I understand why Miss Patience has sequestered herself above stairs. I've seen her with the men in her care and, given her political leanings, she is doing an admirable job."

"Political leanings? What do you know of her political leanings?" I realized that sounded rude. "Sorry, Captain. I didn't expect her to talk to you about politics, or anything else."

"She hasn't spoken to me directly, Miss Becker. Not even when I've spoken to her. She has spoken in my hearing, however."

"Ah." That didn't shock me at all.

"I understand her feelings. That's why I wasn't put out when she sent a slave to care for my men when I asked for a nurse."

"Is your problem her race or her social status?"

He held up a hand. "This isn't about the slave."

"Rosanna knows as much about nursing as Miss Patience, perhaps more. She and her husband took care of old Mister Hamilton before he died." I pushed back my chair. I wanted to get up, move around, walk out the door. "You know black women have been nursing white children, white sick and elderly. Why not white soldiers, too?"

"Enough!"

I pressed my lips together.

"Do you speak this way with the Hamiltons?"

"What would be the point?" I asked, throwing up my hands.

A laugh from across the room proved that Mammy was listening to our conversation.

"But you think there's a point with me?"

I took a calming breath. "Maybe." How could I explain that I wanted him to be more like my father and less like the average officers I had met? "I can hope."

"Perhaps there is a point, but you are missing it in this case. I grew up in a house a lot like this one and my Nanny was darker than Mammy. I never thought she was stupid, or incapable and she would have whooped me if I ever spoke as intemperately as you."

My mother would never whoop me, whatever that entailed, but she would have had words with me. The words would have been short and to the point, like, "Keep. Quiet." I listened to her advice and let the captain get to the point.

"As I was saying, I understand why Miss Patience doesn't want to associate with us damned Yankees. What I don't understand is why she was seen in the vicinity of my men's encampment."

Was she really that stupid?

"I can ask her if you like," I suggested, hoping if I sound stressed it would be attributed to being chastised. "Or, if you can tell me where she was seen, I could hazard a guess. My first thought is that she wanted some fresh air and exercise. Before you arrived, Miss Patience walked every day. Before the horses were taken, she rode almost every day."

"I think I will ask her myself at supper tonight. Would you be so good as to extend my invitation to Mrs. and Miss Hamilton to join us for the evening meal?"

I opened my mouth to object and immediately pursed my lips.

He smiled. "Clever response, Miss Becker. You're learning."

Mama Lou told me that boiling vinegar was almost as good as borax for deterring pests. The room smelled like a pickle barrel when we were done. Compared to the smell of whiskey, stale cigar smoke and the phantom smells of surgery, this was an improvement.

At lunch, I conveyed Captain Stone's invitation. Mrs. Hamilton was gracious about it. Miss Patience was stubborn until I took her aside and pointed out that this came up because she was caught sneaking out to meet Lieutenant Wentworth.

"His hands and feet are raw from the work," she said. "He needs salve and bandages."

"He'll get over it. He won't get over being shot as a spy."

She continued to argue that he was delicate and I was insensitive until I agreed to be her go between. Then, and only then, did she agree to come down for supper.

"You'll have to see all the field hands," Mammy said later.

"I know. It will stand out if I only check up on one."

"You should leave it to Mama Lou."

"I'll get her help, but I promised Patience. Who knows what mischief she'll create if I don't honor my promise."

The nights were getting longer, which meant the bell to call the workers from the field to the evening meal rang earlier. Wentworth should thank his lucky stars that it wasn't summer when the work day was longer, hotter and harder. Mama Lou and I waited for each man, woman and child to wash up, then we inspected their hands, feet, ears and teeth. The ears and teeth were Mama Lou's idea. She remembered having hers checked when she was bought as a child.

Salve and clean bandages were passed out to those who needed them. Other than Wentworth, there were a few children in need. The adults were calloused. Mama Lou also dispensed advice on teeth cleaning and proper washing. For the most part, the advice was taken with respectful good humor. Only Wentworth was put out by the attention, especially when I used his ear examination to tell him that there would be no further visits from Miss Patience.

The process took longer than I expected. I was running late when I headed back to the house. The last thing I needed was a further delay, so naturally one presented itself. Captain Stone's biggest, hardest, scariest sergeant stopped me.

"Miss."

I greeted his grim frown with a polite smile. "Master Sergeant."

He removed his cap and gave me a slight bow. "You know your ranks."

"I started working for Mrs. Hamilton at Fort Leavenworth."

His eyes widened and half his mouth pulled up into a grin. The other half continued to curve down slightly and I realized that his naturally grim expression was caused by damage to his face. "I thought you looked familiar, miss. You have a twin sister, right?'

"You were at Leavenworth? Have we met before?" If it had been before his face was injured, I might not recognize him.

"No, miss. I mean yes, I was at Leavenworth." He scratched his head which had recently been shorn to a black-brown fuzz. "I was a lance corporal back then. But we've never met. Not formally. You and your sister were hard to ignore, though. May I say, you look even prettier than you did back then and that's saying a lot."

"Thank you, Master Sergeant." I turned my feet towards the kitchen door. "I should get going. Your captain is expecting his supper soon."

"Yes, miss. I did have a question for you first. We've seen a few plantations now and not one takes care of their darkies like you do. Not that I'm criticizing. I think it shows good sense and good Christian feeling."

"Thank you," I said, feeling disarmed.

"Thing is, I was wondering if you could inspect my men. We got a hygiene lecture a while back from the committee ladies, but I think some of the boys could use a refresher and it might do more good coming from a pretty nurse like you. You hear what I'm saying?"

"Yes, Master Sergeant." I heard. I wasn't sure if I quite believed what I heard. Did he think I was a nurse? "If it's all right with your captain, Mama Lou and I would be happy to inspect your men."

"Thank you, miss."

I started to leave, then turned back, hoping I wasn't about to give offense. "In the meantime, I'll ask Mama Lou to mix up some tar soap for your men. It does wonders to get rid of fleas and ticks."

"That's very kind of you. Good evening, miss."

Oh what a tangled web I was weaving.

At seven o'clock, I guided Mrs. Hamilton down the main stair case. She had been leaning on me heavily from the attic to the second floor. Once we reached the landing, she straightened her back, lifted her chin and made her final descent with her hand lightly resting on my arm for balance.

Miss Patience stiffly brought up the rear.

The captain and his command staff were waiting in the hall. Usually they would include the senior sergeants in their party. Not this evening.

"Good evening, Miss Becker. Pretty gown."

My dress was blue muslin with a modest hoop, suitable for a paid companion or poor relation. Compared to Mrs. Hamilton's plum satin and Miss Patience's lavender silk, it was a very plain dress, but it was the prettiest dress I owned and I admit, I was pleased he liked it.

"Thank you, Captain Stone." I bobbed a curtsy. "May I present to you Mrs. Hamilton, your host, and Miss Patience Hamilton."

Mrs. Hamilton offered her hand. He took it lightly and bowed over it, a gesture I had not seen since old Mr. Hamilton died.

"May I say, ma'am, you and your daughter are looking lovely tonight."

"Stepdaughter," Patience said.

A slight blush touched Mrs. Hamilton's pale cheeks. I could have swatted Patience.

Captain Stone introduced his officers, acting as if she hadn't spoken.

I'd seen the men before and made a few observations based on their appearance and behavior. Lieutenant Carver was the handsome rogue. With his long blond hair, blue eyes and almost perpetual smirk, he struck me as a man who thought too much of himself. Yet, there must be something to him because he was Captain Stone's second in command.

Carver gave me a nod, then poured on the charm for Mrs. Hamilton and Patience. It took a few minutes before the captain could get to Lieutenant Osmund, who looked so much like the butcher Mama used before we moved to Kansas, I expected him to speak with a German accent. He didn't. It was a little disappointing.

"I know you've met Lieutenant Pickens, Miss Becker."

I offered my hand to Pickens. He was the officer in charge of the supply train. We'd met to discuss supplies and ended up talking about our respective homes. His family were miners, but he had been studying to be a lawyer before he enlisted. He left a fiancée behind. He hoped she'd wait for him.

"It's a pleasure to see you again, miss."

Unlike his fellow officers, he paid little attention to the ladies of the house, to the point of missing a polite question from Mrs. Hamilton. When Captain Stone offered his arm to Mrs. Hamilton, and Carver and Osmund vied with each other to escort Miss Patience, Pickens seemed happy to be my escort to dinner. He was equally happy to offer up no conversation during the meal, which might have been just as well, all things considered.

Mrs. Hamilton took her usual place at one end of the table. Captain Stone sat at the other end. Patience sat in the middle with Carver and Osmund flanking her. Since the table could sit six on each side without the leaves in, she wasn't crowded. Pickens and I had to reach to pass the salt between us.

"I must thank you, Mrs. Hamilton," the captain said, once we were seated. "Miss Becker passed on your message to make use of your wine cellar for tonight's meal."

"Pardon me, Captain?"

"He's thanking you for giving him permission to do what his men have been doing since they arrived," Patience said.

This was absolutely true, but if I could have, I would have kicked her.

"I don't understand what you're saying, Patience. Thaddeus, I trust you have an appropriate selection of wines for the meal?"

"Yes, ma'am."

It was strange to see Thaddeus in the severe black and white suit appropriate for a butler. Haney, the butler I met when I arrived, had been conscripted for labor along with the two footmen. Mama Lou's girls were taking their place, but Mrs. Hamilton insisted on a male butler taking charge.

After a glass of wine and the soup course, Mrs. Hamilton warmed up to her duties as hostess and shared some of the history of Bellevue. This was almost word-for-word the speech old Mr. Hamilton gave guests when he was alive. He was rather deaf and found it easier to lecture than converse at dinner. I'm sure Mrs. Hamilton was copying his behavior so that Patience wouldn't have a chance to say anything dreadful.

"The family is originally from Virginia, you know," she said, after describing the specifications of the plantation. "Well, originally from England, of course, by way of the West Indies. I believe my father-in-law was related to Alexander Hamilton who advised President Washington."

"I thought Alexander Hamilton was from New York," Osmund said. "In fact, I'm sure of it."

"But he was born in St. Croix," Mrs. Hamilton said. "I, myself, am related to the Philadelphia Hamiltons. It was the one thing that made me acceptable to my father-in-law."

Until he found out that the Hamilton family she was related to included the same Andrew Hamilton that defended freedom of the press. Old Mr. Hamilton felt that freedom was something best reserved to the better classes. I looked over at Patience and saw her smirking. She also remembered that moment.

"You're from Philadelphia?" Lieutenant Osmund asked. "So am I."

The atmosphere around the table started to relax. Pickens admitted that he was also from Pennsylvania and missed his home. Carver had a sister in a Massachuset seminary, giving him an opening with Patience. When the entree was served, Captain Stone turned to me.

"Where in New York did you live, Miss Becker?"

"Orange County, close to West Point. My father taught history and Latin. He often tutored officer candidates privately."

"Becker?" Osmund asked. "He helped me cram for my first year exams. I heard he went west. How is the old boy?"

"He died." I didn't say he was killed during the dry-run to this current conflict. "But I'm sure he would have remembered you fondly." He remembered most of his students fondly, even the prats.

"Where are you from, Captain Stone," Mrs. Hamilton asked.

"He's a Texan," Carver said. "He's the black sheep in a very white family, aren't you Captain?"

I glanced over at the captain. His smile didn't bode well for his lieutenant.

"What do you mean, black sheep?" Patience asked Carver.

"Well, the Stone family has its own plantations and slaves but our captain was having none of it."

"Not the Stone family," the captain said softly. "I took my mother's maiden name when I enlisted."

"What is your family name?" Mrs. Hamilton asked, proving that her hearing was fine.

"Doesn't matter. They've pretty much disowned me now."

"That is shameful. Family is family."

"Don't worry, ma'am," Osmund said, patting her hand. "The Stone side is almost as rich and will probably be richer after the war. Next to munitions manufacture, which is my family's business, raising cattle is the next best source of wealth in these times."

"And you, Lieutenant Carver?" Mrs. Hamilton asked. "Are you also from a wealthy family?"

Carver gave a snort of laughter. "No, ma'am. I'm a career soldier. If the rebs don't kill me, the Injuns will. Or maybe the captain will give me a job on his ranch."

"Not if you keep up this line of conversation."

For a moment, my eyes met Captain Stone's. My employer and his subordinates had to be derailed.

"Do you know anything about wine, Captain?" I asked, picking up my half-filled glass. "I don't know a great deal, but this is a Riesling. I have to admit I suggested it to Thaddeus because it's my favorite."

There was a pause. I'd caught him off guard and the others were nonplused. Mrs. Hamilton was frowning at me, but Patience looked grateful for my interruption.

"It's a good choice for pheasant," the captain said. "I can't say I know a lot about wine either, except that reds go best with red meat and whites go best with fish and fowl. My uncle is the wine expert. I enjoy wine with dinner, but I'm more of a beer drinker."

"So was Papa. But he picked grapes to earn his tuition for university. Every time I see a bottle of German wine I wonder if it came from one of the vineyards he worked for."

"If your father was a university student in Germany, I imagine he knew all about beer."

Lieutenant Osmund also knew about beer and took over the conversation, which was fine with me. My work was done.

After dessert, Mrs. Hamilton ushered Patience and myself into the parlor, leaving the men to drink their brandy, smoke and talk about whatever men talked about when ladies were not present. They didn't stay in the dining room long. Either they had enough of male company or the ants were coming out of the woodwork again.

Carver went straight for the pianoforte, a beautiful ebony instrument that took up a corner of the spacious room. He played a couple of chords. I could see Patience white-knuckling her skirt in response.

"I should have paid more attention to my lessons when I had the chance," Carver said. "Do any of you ladies play?"

Walking stiffly, Patience went the piano. Carver pulled the bench out for her. I knew she wasn't going to sit.

"This is my mother's piano. Please do not touch it."

"Will you play then, Mrs. Hamilton?"

"She is not my mother."

Carver gave her a twisted grin. "I never said she was, Miss Patience." Then he bowed graciously to Mrs. Hamilton. "Do you play, ma'am?"

"Not anymore," she said. Not since Miss Patience wouldn't let her touch her dead mother's precious piano, I thought. "But Maggie plays beautifully."

It was my turn to be nonplused. I don't know what surprised me more, being put forward or Mrs. Hamilton standing up to Patience in public. It didn't surprise me at all to see Patience flounce out of the room.

"Please excuse my stepdaughter. She has a headache. Maggie, why don't you play one of those waltzes you used to play all the time."

"Please do," Carver said. "I love to hear other people play."

It didn't take much persuasion. I loved to play and didn't get the opportunity very often. I picked one of my favorite waltzes by Chopin. I'd played it at least once a day for years before coming to Bellevue so I didn't need the sheet music. The piano wasn't perfectly tuned, but I don't think anyone noticed.

One waltz led to another, then I played a polka that was one of my father's favorites. It was a lively tune. At least it started out that way. I remembered playing it while mama and papa danced together and Matty twirled our little brother Werner around until he was out of breath. As I thought about my family, the tempo slowed and by the time I was finished, the Jenny Lind Polka sounded more like a lament.

"I think that's enough," Mrs. Hamilton announced. "It has been a lovely evening, but I am tired, Captain Stone, so I hope you will excuse me if I retire." Once the captain acknowledged her with a bow, she turned to me. "Maggie, will you bring tea to my chamber?"

"Of course, ma'am."

My moment to shine was over. It was time to get back to work.

CHAPTER FOUR

November ended and December settled in with ice cold mornings and bright crisp afternoons. With temporary corrals and paddocks built, the conversion of the stables to barracks and the removal of the last of our patients, everyone had a roof over their heads.

Except when Captain Stone had a meeting, Mrs. Hamilton made a habit of hosting supper for the officers. Since she didn't think that non-commissioned officers belonged at the family table, the summer parlor was designated as the Sergeants' Mess.

Patience was not allowed to bow out of the gatherings and further outbursts were not tolerated. It didn't take me long to figure out why Mrs. Hamilton had put her foot down. She had set her sights on the captain as a prospective son-in-law.

"It'll be a cold day in Hell when that happens," Mammy said, when I shared my theory. We were peeling carrots and potatoes for the evening meal, being very generous with the peels since they would be going into Mama Lou's stew pot. "I know Mrs. Hamilton means well, but just her wanting Miss Patience to be sweet to Captain Stone will guarantee she acts as sour as a pickle."

"Sweet is asking a lot, but I suggested that being pleasant was for the greater good."

"And she listened to you?"

I laughed. "She listened when I reminded her that the greater good included the welfare of her beloved Nathaniel."

Mammy snorted, then shook her head in warning. She might be getting old and stiff but her hearing was excellent. She always knew when we were about to be interrupted. Not that she always warned me. I think she delighted in letting Captain Stone startle me.

"Good morning, Miss Becker. Keeping well, I hope, Mammy."

"Well as can be. Miss Maggie, why don't you let Labelle take over and you pour the captain a fresh cup of coffee."

Yes, the captain had thoroughly charmed my elderly friend. I wiped my hands on my apron and followed orders.

"What can I do for you, Captain?" I asked.

Don't get me wrong. I was happy to have Captain Stone's company for a second time in one morning. I was growing very partial to his company. That didn't stop me from questioning his presence during his usual time for doing paperwork in his office.

"I just received a dispatch. Colonel Redmond will be joining us for dinner. He's bringing a few staff officers, his wife and daughter. Oh, and he's looking forward to meeting the Hamiltons."

"Tonight?"

"I'm afraid so. If it's any help, Colonel Redmond sent supplies ahead. Pickens will be delivering them shortly. They include sugar, flour, tea and," he paused, "coffee."

"Coffee?"

"I knew that would perk you up."

I winced, which produced a happy grin from Captain Stone. How could I help but return it.

"Also, knowing that you'd be busy, I've already talked to Mrs. Hamilton and she won't need you to serve her lunch today. She's even offered to help with arrangements."

Dropping a shallow curtsey, I thanked him. Not long after, I would curse that particular kindness.

"I'm torn," Mrs. Hamilton said while Rosanna and two girls lowered her gown over her head and arranged the skirt over her hoop. "I rely on you, Maggie, to ensure everything goes smoothly. Without Haney, not to mention a proper chef, I'd like you in charge of the kitchen."

I tried not to grimace. It wasn't that I particularly wanted to be part of the formal dinner, but I didn't quite trust Patience to behave. In any case, Mammy had already kicked me out of the kitchen saying that she and Labelle had everything under control.

"On the other hand," she continued, "the numbers are going to be uneven enough with so many men attending."

"I think she should be at the table," Patience said, surprising both of us. "It's going to seem odd otherwise. If nothing else, Captain Stone will wonder why she's suddenly unwelcome."

"Oh no, not unwelcome," Mrs. Hamilton said, turning about the look at me. This caused some frustration for her dressers. "You know I value you highly, don't you Maggie?"

"Yes, ma'am, of course." I brought her sash, ready for when she was laced into her gown. "Truly, there is nothing left for me to do in the kitchen. I could help with the service, as I did when I first came to work for you, but I think that might seem a little odd now."

"Very odd," Patience said. "There's no need, either. Thaddeus has brought in extra help. You've turned Maggie into your lieutenant. You can't very well change her status now."

We both stared at Patience in disbelief.

"Very well," Mrs. Hamilton said, once the shock wore off. "You had better change your dress then, Maggie. I think you should wear the grey one. No need to call attention to yourself."

Nothing I owned called attention to me, especially in the company of the lovely Patience. My grey poplin gown was very plain, almost severe. It made me feel years older to wear it. I suppose wasn't a bad thing these days. The effect was ruined when Captain Stone made me laugh.

"I'm sorry, did someone die?"

"Many good men have died, Stone. And many good women have lost family and friends."

The man speaking was Colonel Redmond. Even if I had not recognized his rank insignia, I would have known him as the ranking officer present by his bearing.

The woman beside Redmond pinched his arm. "The Captain was teasing, George. By now, I'm sure he's on good enough terms with the family to get away with that. Though introductions would be welcome first."

"Quite right, my dear." The colonel didn't lose an ounce of his aplomb. "Stone, you've met my wife Abigail and I think you've met Mrs. Hepburn."

The captain had been taken aback, but he made a quick recovery.

"It is a pleasure to finally meet you, Mrs. Hamilton," Redmond said, when the introductions were concluded. "Your cooperation in these trying times has been exemplary."

Patience bit her lip. I know she wanted to speak up, but she didn't.

"These are trying circumstances," Mrs. Hamilton said. "Yours are not the first troops to occupy our home. I fear you may not be the last." She laid a hand on the colonel's arm. "Captain Stone, will you escort Mrs. Redmond? I believe we have time for a sherry before dinner."

Lieutenants Carver and Osmund both offered an arm to Patience.

"I think I'll pull rank," one of Redmond's aides said, nudging both aside. "Captain Honeywell, at your service miss."

Honeywell was almost as old as the colonel, but in fairness, almost as handsome as Captain Stone. Patience dropped a demure curtsey and gave Honeywell her hand. Carver and Osmund brought up the rear in close order.

Lieutenant Pickens, as usual, offered me his arm. We followed Captain and Mrs. Hepburn into the parlor. Waiting for us, with a tray of tiny glasses, was Nathaniel Wentworth.

My knees buckled.

"Are you alright, Miss Maggie?" Pickens whispered, steadying me.

"Lost my footing," I lied. Nate offered the tray. Normally I don't drink. I took a glass and tossed it back. "I'll be fine."

It was the longest dinner in creation.

Nate shuffled about, keeping his head down, but I caught him giving the younger officers dark looks whenever they paid attention to Patience. Fortunately, Thaddeus kept him too busy to lurk and draw attention to himself. Not for one moment did I believe that it was Thaddeus's idea to bring him in.

There was worse to come after dessert.

When Mrs. Hamilton rose to lead the ladies into the parlor, Colonel Redmond cleared his throat noisily.

"Would you ladies indulge me by staying a moment longer?"

Mrs. Hamilton paused, neither sitting nor leaving the table.

"I have a letter for you from Major Hamilton."

She sat.

He turned to Hepburn. "Fetch my dispatch case." Smiling, he turned his attention back to Mrs. Hamilton. "I know you will want to read your husband's message as soon as possible, so we will not trespass on your hospitality much longer. Before we take our leave, I have one small piece of business to address."

I shot Captain Stone a questioning look. With a fraction rise to his shoulder and the tiniest shake of the head, he conveyed that he didn't know what was coming.

"You have cotton and tobacco in your storage sheds. It won't last much longer without rotting."

I bit the inside of my cheeks. Patience had vowed she'd rather burn the lot than let the Yankees get hold of Bellevue's crop. I had convinced her to trade it to local merchants, in small quantities, for goods we needed. I'd done a little trading myself with Pickens—tobacco for coffee.

"We could appropriate it," Redmond continued. "We'd rather maintain friendlier relations. After all, Tennessee never seceded. We don't need to be enemies."

"And yet, sir, my husband is in a Union prison. Would he approve of such a transaction?"

"Approve, maybe not. Enjoy the benefit of cooperation, perhaps."

Nate moved in to stand behind Patience. I could hardly blame him. Patience had a strangle hold on her wine glass. I was afraid it would break in her hand.

I cleared my throat. "I'm sure the colonel is not suggesting that Major Hamilton is in any danger if you refuse to comply, only that he will be relieved that his wife and daughter are in no danger from the occupying forces."

Redmond didn't like me using the phrase, "occupying forces" but he was canny enough not to say anything. I also suspect that Mrs. Redmond kicked him under the table.

Patience relaxed a little and put the wine glass down. "Colonel, you will give us some time to consider, won't you? We must, after all, balance our needs against the wishes of my father." Her tone was honeyed, true southern belle. "In the meantime, I think we can continue to trade tobacco with your troops and provide cotton lint to your medics."

I bit my lip. She knew more than I gave her credit for.

"I have a wonderful idea," she said. "We should have a Christmas Ball. It will give us a chance to meet your other officers and allow us to be social with our neighbors again. My step-mama and I will confer and give you our decision then."

"Excellent idea," Mrs. Hamilton said, not too sincerely.

I had a bad feeling the cotton was going to go up in flames Christmas Eve.

CHAPTER FIVE

I wasn't the only one who was mistrustful of Patience. The next morning, when Patience went out walking, Mrs. Hamilton sent Junie down to the kitchen to fetch me.

Junie was one of the girls Mama Lou had sent into the house to keep out of the way of the soldiers. Mrs. Hamilton had taken to the child and recently adopted her as a personal servant. Junie took the place I had filled when I first worked for the family. Unlike me, she wasn't a bit shy and she ran into the kitchen shouting for me.

"Miss Maggie! Miss Mag—" She clapped a hand over her mouth and skidded to a stop when she saw Captain Stone was in the kitchen, sitting with me at the table.

The captain was startled by her reaction. I was torn between amusement and concern.

"Junie, is Mrs. Hamilton unwell?"

"No," she mumbled through her hand.

"Then take a take a breath, take your hand away from your mouth, and give me your message."

"The Missus wants you upstairs now. She says it's important. You shouldn't wait case Missy Patience comes back."

That wasn't the least bit suspicious, was it?

I told Junie to run up and tell Mrs. Hamilton I was coming, then I let my head fall and shook it a couple of times.

"I'm guessing they are at outs again," I said. "They often are and I am put in the middle of it."

"I noticed," Captain Stone said. "I've also noticed that Miss Patience is taking a greater interest in my officers."

"Well, you took away her patients. She's getting restless."

"Is that all it is?"

I didn't want to lie. I liked Captain Stone. A lot. He treated the household with more respect than I could have hoped and, had I not been bound to the Hamiltons, I would have been on his side in this conflict. I hedged.

"Mrs. Hamilton has expressed the opinion that you would be a good match. She's pushing Patience to be...to be nice."

I should have waited until he swallowed his coffee. When he stopped choking, I excused myself to attend Mrs. Hamilton.

Half an hour later, I returned to the kitchen having promised my mistress that I would keep an eye on her stepdaughter. Captain Stone had left the house, which was to be expected but still disappointing.

"If there's still coffee in the pot, why don't you pour us some and set a spell," Mammy said.

I shook my head. "I have to go find Miss Patience."

"No you don't. She came looking for the captain a while back and talked him into taking her riding."

I pursed my lips to stop myself from saying something unladylike.

"Pour the coffee child and set. Miss Patience is up to something but it isn't stealing the captain from you. Not that she could if she tried."

Flustered, I dropped my cup. One of the new kitchen girls rushed over to sweep up before I had my senses about me.

"That was my favorite," I said, just staring at the floor where it hit. I forced a smile for the girl, who was cringing, as if I would blame her for my clumsiness. "Thank you."

Mammy was supervising two more girls as they peeled potatoes. She shooed them away when I sat down with her. "There's so many of these chits running around now, it's all I can do not to trip over them. Got to keep them busy too, or they start making eyes at the young men."

"The soldiers?"

"More like the comely boys recruited for house staff, including Mr. Nate." She snorted. "I wonder if Miss Patience thought of that when she brought him in."

"Probably not." Just like she hadn't realized that Nate would come under my control in the house. She wasn't happy when I put him on polishing duty. He was part of a small posse of young men who escaped labor conscription last spring. When they were done cleaning the brass and silver, there were lamps to be cleaned and the crystals in the chandeliers to be polished until they glittered. The proposed ball gave me an excuse, and Mrs. Hamilton gave me her blessing.

"So, young lady, I'm guessing that Mrs. Hamilton still wants Captain Stone for Miss Patience. I wonder how the Master would feel about that or about this cotton deal they're considering. Has the missus confided what's in the letter she got sent?"

"Not exactly. She says he wants her to stay safe and take care of Patience. I think she takes that as permission to match-make, but I know she's uncomfortable with selling cotton. She'd rather the army confiscate it. Then there would be no question of collaboration."

Mammy snorted. "Not that her back got broke bringing in that crop. I'd rather you keep trading bits and pieces for the things we need to keep body and soul together."

"She's also worried about what the neighbors will say. She's always been an outsider. She doesn't want to be seen as a traitor, too."

"But she wants to marry off her stepdaughter to an enemy officer."

"A rich officer," I pointed out. "It would seem that wealth conquers politics. I hope for Nate's sake, love conquers all."

Although Captain Stone had given his permission almost immediately, both Master Sergeant and I had been too busy for a health inspection of the troops. With winter upon us, not to mention the shared risk if there was an outbreak of disease, Mama Lou and I decided it was time to make good on my promise.

Patience unbent enough to agree to see anyone needing nursing. It was truly amazing how many stomach aches had developed overnight. Very few actually required her attention. What they needed, more than anything, was Mamma Lou's homemade tooth powder. There were not many sweet breaths in the ranks. In the balance, most of them had made use of soap and water both to clean themselves and their uniforms. Beards were trimmed and hair slicked down. It really brought home how young most of them were.

Later, when Master Sergeant and I sat for a cup of tea in Mamma Lou's kitchen, I complimented him on his men. I could have also mentioned that he was looking much better, now that his hair was growing in, thick, shiny and insect free.

"I'd say your hygiene efforts are paying off."

He barked a laugh. "More like the notion of being seen by young ladies paid off. Besides, we're not foot soldiers. We take pride in our appearance when we can."

I remembered seeing the cavalry troops strut about at the fort and knew he was right. Cavalry officers, in particular, were rather vain that way. The only thing they put above their appearance was the wellbeing of their horses.

"How are the horses?" I asked. "Thaddeus is very good with animals, especially horses. I know you all are, but he has the gift. Like Mama Lou does with people."

"That explains a lot. He's avoided my men as much as possible. For that matter, my men avoid him, too. But he's been seen around the corral. No offense, but what we really could use is a farrier. We lost ours to the rebs."

"So did we. They took him with our horses."

We shared a moment of silent mutual sympathy.

"Thaddeus worked with him," I said. "He is a free man, you know. Thaddeus, not the farrier."

"Your farrier was a slave?" He sounded shocked and possibly appalled by the news.

"Just about everyone that works at Bellevue, short of a few field overseers who are gone now thank heavens, are slaves. The exceptions are Thaddeus and myself. And we're not as free as we'd like to be, I must admit."

He stared at me, obviously puzzled. "But a plantation this size..."

"Needs a butcher, a baker, a candlestick maker. When I arrived, we also had a carpenter, blacksmith and farrier. All slaves."

After digesting this information for a minute, he asked the inevitable question. "Then what do the white folk do?"

"You mean the ones who don't own the plantations?"

He nodded.

"The skilled workers do the same jobs in town for a decent wage, I hope. Out here, they hire out during the planting and harvest. No plantation can possibly keep enough slaves, year round, to bring in the harvest. Extra workers and overseers are needed. They move from place to place as needed. Some have their own farms to tend as well. My father used to say it's been the same since feudal times. Slaves and serfs aren't very different." When he shot me a puzzled frown I explained. "My father was a teacher and a history scholar. He made sure that my sister and I were well-read."

"If your father was a teacher, how did you end up here?"

I was getting used to answering this question. Major Hamilton had asked it when he hired me. Captain Stone had extracted the story in bits and pieces since we met.

"My father and mother came to America from Germany. My father's scholarship wasn't as well-respected here, but he taught in a boy's school when we were growing up. He also tutored West Point students."

Master Sergeant gave one of lopsided smiles. "Bet they needed it."

"They did. We did all right, but papa wanted us to have something we could all build on. So he took us to homestead in Kansas."

"Oh." I think he saw the next bit coming because the sergeant was suddenly somber.

"You probably know about the raids across the Missouri border by men who wanted Kansas to be a slave state."

He nodded.

"My father was killed in one of the raids. He was a vocal abolitionist. He was killed at political meeting and our farm was attacked and burned shortly after. That's when our mother took us to live near Fort Leavenworth. She taught piano and took in laundry. My sister Matty and

I went into service. Which, of course, you know."

"I know. You do what you have to for your family. That's why I joined up. It's worked out for me, but it was a hard row to hoe when I left my home."

I wanted to ask why he had to leave home, but he didn't give me the chance.

"The Army is my home now. Those boys are my family. I'm supposing the people here are like family to you, too. That's why you take good care of them."

He looked down at his empty cup but waved off my offer to pour him more tea. A shiver shot up my spine, anticipation of trouble coming.

"From one family protector to another, I need to give you a warning," he said, pitch and volume low. "Miss Patience has been seen by our patrols further from the house than she has any business going unaccompanied. I spotted her once in the company of a man. I'm thinking she might have a suitor in the area and I'm hoping he isn't a reb. We've spotted scouts. Mostly we've been leaving them alone just as they're leaving ours alone. No one wants a battle right now. But if she's passing information..."

"I'm sure she's not," I interjected. "She has many friends in the neighborhood. Were these meetings at night?"

"No, miss."

"Was she on horseback? I understand Captain Stone lets her ride."

He nodded. "Maybe she should have an escort to make sure she's safe."

I bit my lip. It was not my place to agree or disagree to this suggestion. Truth to tell, I wasn't sure what I would say in any case.

I pushed back my stool, cuing us both to stand. "Thank you for taking tea with me, sergeant. I had better get back to work now."

He offered me his hand.

"You do what you have to for your family, Miss Maggie. If you need my help, I'll give it if I can."

"Thank you. I'll remember that." And I prayed I wouldn't have to take him up on his offer.

That evening, we had our first family evening in weeks. Captain Stone and his officers were dining at a neighboring plantation. Lieutenant Pickens was left behind as the Officer of the Day. He dined with us, then took himself, and a bottle of whisky, to join the sergeants' mess.

It was a pleasant meal, almost like before the war. A little part of me felt guilt for enjoying the benefits of the Union occupation. Not for my part, of course. Given a choice, I was for the Union cause, especially now that President Lincoln was emancipating the slaves. But Major

Hamilton had entrusted me with the care of his wife and daughter, even to teaching me how to load and shoot a pistol. I wasn't bad either, though not as good a shot as Patience. In his way, he was as enlightened as Papa in thinking that young women needed to be educated. And that's where the guilt stemmed.

Was I betraying the major's trust by negotiating their collaboration with their enemy? Was their security, and my inclination, just cause?

"Maggie, is there something wrong? I've asked you twice to pour the tea."

"Sorry, Mrs. Hamilton."

We were sitting in the parlor. The sound of laughter and off-key singing could be heard from across the entry hall, despite the two sets of closed doors.

I poured the tea and noticed that Patience was almost as distracted as me. Unfortunately, Mrs. Hamilton also noticed.

"Nathaniel didn't serve dinner tonight," she said. "I didn't want to mention in front of Lieutenant Pickens, but I was wondering about that."

"I forgot that Thaddeus left to go hunting and told him he could take the evening off," Patience said. "Maggie has been working him ragged. In fact, I'd like to retire early tonight as well."

"We'll all retire after tea," Mrs. Hamilton said. "But I'd like a little of your time first, Patience. I want to go over the guest list one more time."

I bit the inside of my cheek to stop myself from grinning. If Patience had any idea of slipping off to meet Nate, she wasn't going to get the chance. One less thing for me to worry about.

It was getting noisier in the other room.

"Perhaps we should take our tea upstairs," I suggested. The volume increased significantly. The party was spilling into the entry hall. "And maybe we should take the back stairs."

Mrs. Hamilton nodded and pushed herself out of her chair just as the door from the hall was thrust open with a wood splintering crash.

"Lieutenant Pickens!" If Mrs. Hamilton was afraid, it was well hidden by outrage. "If you wanted to come in, you could have turned the door knob. A gentle knock, to announce yourself would have been appropriate. This is not."

"Sorry, ma'am," he said, slurring his esses. "I guess my hand slipped." Behind him, one of the men giggled. "If you're heading to bed, don't let us stop you. Just need Miss Maggie here to play us a song or two on your p'yano...pee-ann-oh."

Mrs. Hamilton threw out her chest like an angry peacock. "You are drunk, sir. Your conduct is unbecoming. I suggest you get some fresh air and sober up before your commander returns."

This wasn't the first inebriated junior officer Mrs. Hamilton had scolded. This may have been the first time she'd done so when help was not a call away. There was no senior officer here, or garrison guard. Only a handful of non-commissioned officers who were at least as drunk as the lieutenant.

"Perhaps you and Patience should leave," I said. "I don't mind playing the piano for a little while. Captain Stone and the other officers are sure to be back soon."

"I think we should keep the pretty one to dance with," a corporal said, pushing his way to the front of the group.

Pickens shook his head. "I want Maggie to play 'Lorena.' Or 'Weeping Sad and Lonely.'"

"No, let's have a dance instead," the corporal said.

Pickens pulled out his pistol and whipped the man across the face with its butt. The other soldiers backed away. Then he pointed the gun at Patience.

"Put that poker down, Miss Hamilton. I'm drunk, not blind. Sit down, ladies. Except you, Miss Maggie. I need you to play."

I looked around. Patience had armed herself with a fire iron. She was now putting it down. Mrs. Hamilton was looking pale and not nearly as proud as before. Patience helped her sit on the settee and sat beside her, holding her stepmother's hand. The part of me that wasn't scared to death was touched by this.

"What's going on, Lieutenant?" I asked as I took my seat at the piano.

He peered at me, "What?"

"What's happened?"

"Nothing. Just play 'Lorena.'"

"I don't have the music for that song."

"Play," he insisted, turning the pistol on me.

I had heard the soldiers singing 'Lorena,' so I tried picking out the tune by ear and found myself playing a German folk song instead. It was the first piece Mama taught me. That tune flowed naturally into another traditional song that could have been danced to at the right tempo. I gave it the pace and chords of a lament. I did the same with a military march.

"More," he said loudly when I stopped.

"That's enough, Peter."

I looked around. The drunken soldiers were gone. So were Mrs. Hamilton and Patience. Captain Stone had returned. He took the pistol from Pickens' now slack grip.

"Put him to bed, Clive. And keep an eye on him."

Lieutenant Osmund took Pickens by the elbow and led him away. When the door closed behind them, Captain Stone took me by the elbow and led me to the settee.

"I'm going to see if there's any tea left in the pot," he said. There was. He fortified it with some brandy before handing me the cup. "That should help."

The tea was cold, but the brandy burned. I had to hold the cup with both hands, which was odd since my hands were steady enough when I was playing.

"I don't understand," I said, not quite sure what I was referring to. Maybe everything. "Where are Mrs. Hamilton and Miss Patience? Where are the men who were here? And the one Lieutenant Pickens knocked out? Why didn't I hear you come in? What happened?"

"Did he hurt you?"

"He waved a gun in my face." I finished the cup and thrust it at him. "He threatened to shoot Patience. Only I'm allowed to do that."

The captain smiled, but it quickly faded.

"Forgive Peter. He's a good man. He had the kind of courage that inspired the men under him. He was promoted for that as much as his brave actions. But war takes its toll on men. Some more than others."

I always thought Lieutenant Pickens was a good man. That's what made his actions so shocking. I looked down in my lap. My hands were still shaking. For the life of me I couldn't tell how much was fear and how much anger.

Captain Stone covered my hands with his. "I'm so sorry you had to see this side of the man, and so proud of the way you handled the situation. Even under duress, you played beautifully."

"When did you get back?" I asked.

"Less than a half hour ago. One of the more sensible men left the house to find Master Sergeant. He found me first. He told me Pickens was armed, so I came in quietly." He squeezed my hands. "He was so mesmerized by you, and you were so caught up with playing, neither of you noticed my arrival. I had Carver quietly escort Mrs. and Miss Hamilton upstairs."

"And the other men?"

"Pickens was the only one in the room."

I shook my head. "There were four others. All drunk. Pickens pistol whipped one of them for arguing with him."

"One of them tried to stop Pickens?"

"No." I pulled my hands away and started pacing. "One of them wanted to force Patience to dance with them. Pickens wanted sad music. What happened to him?"

He shook his head, slow and tired. "I told you. War. You wouldn't understand"

"I've seen what war can do, Captain."

He caught up to my pacing and grabbed my shoulders. A flash of memory, of being roughly grabbed by one of the men who attacked our farm, brought back that feeling of panic at being overpowered. I don't know who pulled him away from me, or how I managed to run away. It seemed like such a small victory in the face of the loss of papa and our home.

"You've seen the physical effects. You haven't seen how it wears a soul down." His fingers bit into my flesh. "You tasted fear tonight. Feed on it day in and day out for months on end. You have no idea. You will never have any idea. I thank God for that." I looked up into eyes as grey as ashes. There was no running away tonight.

"I'm going to make coffee, Captain. Would you like a cup? Mammy swears by tea but I find I need coffee to wash down fear. This isn't my first taste. Not by a long shot."

He let go. Shame suffused his face.

Good.

I turned on my heel and retreated to the kitchen.

CHAPTER SIX

I didn't see Captain Stone for coffee the next morning. I shouldn't have cared, or been surprised. Nevertheless, I poked my head into the dining room to see if he was at the table with his officers.

He wasn't. Neither was Pickens.

Osmund saw me. "Miss Maggie?"

"Sorry to bother you, Lieutenant. I was just looking for Nate. I had an errand for him."

"Last I saw him, he was polishing boots. That boy's got a real knack for it. They let darkies into the cavalry and he'd make a great batman."

I bit my tongue, partly to keep from laughing.

"I think Miss Patience has him," Carver said. "She wanted him to saddle a horse for her. I offered to help her, but she's a bit shy of us today."

"She shouldn't be riding alone," Osmund said.

"If the boy's with her, she's not alone. Face it, Clive, we're going to have some work to charm her back after last night."

I ducked back into the kitchen.

There were a lot of chores that I could do, but not that many that needed my personal attention. Junie would fetch Mrs. Hamilton's breakfast in an hour or so. It was doubtful I would be called to attend her. If Thaddeus was here, I'd send him to check on Patience, but I could hardly ask anyone else.

"Mammy, can you think of a good reason I might want to go to the corral?"

The girls working beside her giggled. Mammy gave them the eye and they stopped, pressing their lips together in tight lines.

"Do you have a good reason?"

"Yes. But I need one that I can tell the troopers if I get stopped."

Mammy pulled a knobby tipped parsnip out of the barrel and inspected it. One of the girls snorted, then both of them almost swallowed their lips to stifle their laughter when Mammy said, "Tell 'em you want to ride. It worked for Miss Patience."

This wasn't a brilliant idea. Unlike Patience, I didn't have a riding habit or boots. For that matter, the last horse I rode was the big brute we had for pulling the plow on weekdays and taking us to church on Sundays. On the other hand, I didn't have a better plan. But maybe I had an ally.

I knocked on the door of the Sergeant's Mess and asked for Master Sergeant. He was the type to do a half-day's work before breakfast so he could linger over coffee. I'm positive that, had he been around the night before, the incident with Lieutenant Pickens would never have happened.

"Miss Maggie?"

Concerned brown eyes gazed down at me. Beyond his broad shoulders, I could see the smirking face of one of the corporals that had accompanied Perkins into the parlor.

"Master Sergeant, I need to consult with you on a matter of camp hygiene."

His eyes brows lifted, but he nodded and followed me outside.

The sun was making short work of the evening's frost. I only wished it could burn away the effects of Pickens's outburst as easily.

"Something wrong, Miss Maggie?"

I hesitated.

"Is it about last night?"

It wasn't. I nodded anyway.

He looked over his shoulder towards the house, then took my elbow and led me into the walled garden.

Old Mrs. Hamilton, the Major's mother, had designed the garden based on a book she'd read. When I first came to Bellevue, it bloomed eight months of the year. The poor woman was probably turning in her grave now.

Bellevue had a kitchen garden, of course, and a couple of the fields had been turned from cash crops to root vegetables like potatoes, beets and turnips. Still, my father's stories about the hardships of wartime haunted me. Enemy or ally, it didn't make much difference to the German peasants whose winter stores were stolen by soldiers living off the land. This is why I suggested hiding produce in the flower beds. To his credit, Major Hamilton listened to me and gave the orders to make it so, with one proviso. His mother's roses and imported perennials had to be preserved.

Roses still climbed the garden wall, leaves all but fallen and hips picked clean for preserves and tea, but they were interspersed with onions and garlic. The center beds were almost entirely given over to herbs and vegetables, but the remaining flowers and ornamental hedges kept up the illusion of an English style garden. They also masked the view from the house.

Master Sergeant directed me to one of the garden benches. Sitting, we were hidden from view of the main drive. This made me a little nervous.

"Are you worried the men involved won't be punished?" he asked, point blank. "I've identified three men that were with the Lieutenant. The one with a lump on his head was the easiest. They've been docked pay, given extra guard duty and lost their privileges to use the parlor you so generously set aside for us."

"One of them was at the house this morning. The sandy-haired corporal, but not the one who came to the door."

"You're sure."

I nodded. "I'm sure. He leered at me much the same way as he did last night."

Master Sergeant's lips pursed and his head dropped. Then he looked heavenward, as if asking for God's strength.

"I'll take care of him."

"And what of Lieutenant Pickens?"

"That's up to the Captain."

I interlaced my fingers to keep myself from wringing my hands.

"He'll do what's best, miss. Pickens just has to be kept away from hard drinking. So do I, for that matter."

He chuckled at the way I stared at him. I suppose I went a little bug-eyed at his admission. Captain Stone's affliction was catching.

"Whiskey breaks down the walls we build around our feelings. That's not always such a bad thing. You just got to know when to stop. Men like me and Pickens aren't so good at stopping once we get going. When the wall comes down, Pickens sees dead and dismembered bodies, and he mourns."

"How about you?"

"I see the enemy and need to kill him before he kills any more of my men." This time his laugh held no mirth. "Trust me. You're better off with Pickens drunk than me."

"Then I trust I'll never see you drunk, Master Sergeant. And I sincerely hope you never see me as your enemy." I felt my clenched hands pressing into my lap and willed them to relax. "My father used to say, "Don't paint the Devil on the wall." It means, don't invite trouble. I'm worried I might be doing just that."

He grinned. "By discussing hygiene with me?"

"By discussing anything with you in a private place." I stood, shaking my hands out and rolling my shoulders to ease the tension in them. Not the most ladylike gestures. "I shouldn't have let myself get sidetracked. The reason I sought you out was to see if you had anyone accompanying Miss Patience on her ride today, or if she took one of the servants."

Master Sergeant pushed himself to his feet. A frown pulled his brows together into a straight line above narrowed eyes.

"I wasn't aware of her taking a horse out," he said, all business now. "I can find out if anyone went with her. What are you worried about?"

"I don't know. She could be home safe and sound now, for all I know." I rubbed my eyes. Another unladylike gesture. "I just want to know she's safe."

"Then let's find out."

He strode off towards the corral with me half running to keep up. When we got there, I let him do all the talking. I was out of breath.

"She rode off with one of her darkies," the corporal in charge said. "The Captain said she could ride Ginger, right?"

"That's what he said. But it's my job to keep everyone secure so, from now on, you let me know when she's going out."

"Yes, Master Sergeant."

"Saddle Chalk and that chestnut there. Miss Maggie and me are going to ride out and meet Miss Patience."

"We are?" I squeaked.

"You want to ride sidesaddle, Miss?" the corporal asked. "I think there's a lady's saddle in the tack room."

"Absolutely not." Having only ridden astride a farm horse, I couldn't imagine staying seated without being able to grip with both knees.

Master Sergeant patted me on the shoulder. "I'm going to let you ride Chalk. He's mine and the calmest mount I've ever had. No need to be scared."

I just nodded. I wasn't scared of horses. I was very appreciative of their efforts in pulling plows and carts and enjoyed feeding them apples as a reward. I was a bit nervous about riding.

My, cavalry troopers were efficient at saddling those big brutes.

Master Sergeant laced his fingers and crouched down. "Just put your foot here, and one hand on my shoulder. I'll throw you into the saddle. You just have to grab the horn and swing your leg over."

I followed the directions and was rewarded by the exhilarating sensation of feeling light as a feather as I was effortlessly tossed up. Then my crinoline, not being designed for saddles, popped up like an umbrella in a high wind.

"Master Sergeant, what the hell are you doing?"

I pushed my skirt down and saw Captain Stone, red-faced and fists clenched, and Master Sergeant looking very, very pale.

Because it was the worst possible timing, Patience rode up.

"What are you doing, Maggie? Surely you have better things to do than make a spectacle of yourself."

Tempted to pull my skirt back up over my face, I attempted to dismount instead. The hem of my underdress caught on something and an ominous ripping sound broke the awkward silence. I reached around to free myself and started to fall. I thought Master Sergeant was closest, but it was Captain Stone that caught me.

"Her skirt is tangled on the cantle. Get it free, Master Sergeant." As soon as I was disentangled, he set me down. It was only then that I realized we had attracted an audience. "Miss Becker, now that I know you are interested in learning to ride, I will try to arrange a more suitable teacher...someone with sisters, who knows the difference between a day dress and a riding habit."

"I doubt she'll have time," Patience said, beckoning me to her like a trained dog. "There are so many preparations left to take care of for the Christmas Eve Ball. When she does have time, she should spend it practicing the piano. We're counting on her to play."

"Unnecessary. I've invited the regimental band to play before dinner and Mrs. Hamilton informs me that she has engaged musicians for the dance. Now, I am sure Mrs. Hamilton is expecting you ladies for lunch." He gave us a shallow bow. "Don't let me detain you."

Patience looked like she wanted to spit, but she made a dignified exit. I tried to do the same while trailing a torn flounce.

"What were you thinking?" Patience hissed.

I waited until we were well out of earshot. "What were you thinking? Your solitary rides are being noticed. If anyone finds out your going off to meet Nate..."

She stopped to stomp her foot.

"Whether or not I meet Nathaniel is none of your concern."

"You asked me to take care of Nate. And before you get on your high horse, he gave me permission to use that name."

She bristled but pursed her lips against another outburst.

I continued. "Your father told me to take care of you and your stepmother. So yes, it is my concern. If you have any regard for the safety of your stepmother, or any of us, you will take care."

"Fine," she said, and headed to the front entrance.

"Fine," I echoed, heading for the kitchen door. I tripped on my petticoat. "Just fine."

CHAPTER SEVEN

When Mrs. Hamilton summoned me to join her for tea, I expected the worst. It was worse than I expected.

"I hear you have a beau, my dear."

"A beau?"

"You were seen walking out with one of Captain Stone's sergeants. Of course, it's a little awkward with him being an enemy soldier, but otherwise it is an eminently suitable match." She patted my hand. "Nevertheless, I must caution you to take care. You can't let your affections get in the way of your duties, or his. I understand that he got into a little trouble with Captain Stone over you."

I nodded. What else could I do?

"Well, dear, I know that the Captain has taken a friendly interest in you, and I'm sure he only wants what is best. He has a duty to maintain the integrity of his command. However, I'm sure the sergeant has some time off every day, and so long as it isn't at an unseemly or inconvenient hour, I will allow you to take some time off."

I responded automatically. "Thank you, ma'am."

"Perhaps Captain Stone can speak to his master sergeant about scheduling."

"I was with Master Sergeant."

She patted my hand again and beamed. "Well done, dear. A very suitable match. Perhaps I'll invite him to join us for supper."

I had a pistol, and I knew how to use it. The question was, should I shoot Mrs. Hamilton or myself?

Someone had to suffer for my day. Nate showed up at just the right, or wrong moment. He was supervising the laying of the table, with an extra place set. It didn't help my temper to see the girls taking direction from him as if they had never laid out cutlery and plates before.

"You. With me. Now."

He didn't balk until I had him in private in the butler's pantry, then he was more puzzled than anything.

"What's wrong?"

"You. Patience. Everything." I took a calming breath. I hadn't shouted, but I was worked up and screaming was only a breath away. "You can't keep meeting Patience on the sly. Do you think you're the only one who would be shot as a spy?"

Nate laid his hands on my shoulders and gave them a squeeze. "I haven't been meeting Patience. I kept my promise, Maggie. If this is about the errand she had me run this morning, she was only trying to give me a break from all the work." He grinned down at me. "She's never been dogsbody to a colonel or she'd know the chores you give me around the house are nothing in comparison."

"I don't understand. She didn't ride off with you?"

He shook his head. "She probably took one of the boys with her as a groom. It wouldn't be proper for a lady to be out riding without as escort."

I stared at him awhile. "She's been seen meeting someone."

His hands clenched on my shoulders. "Not me."

"If not you..."

The door from the dining room opened. I pulled away from Nate. It wouldn't do to have the girls gossiping about us.

"Miss Becker?" It was Captain Stone.

Nate hurried out through the kitchen.

Great. As if the situation didn't look bad enough.

I forced a smile. "Coffee? It's my brew, not real coffee. I'm saving the real coffee for the party. I want you and Mrs. Hamilton to make a good impression. It does have some grounds in it. The coffee I'm brewing now, that is. They add flavor." I stopped babbling and tried to smile again.

He shook his head and walked away.

There were two empty place settings at dinner. Lieutenant Pickens, Captain Stone reported, was still feeling under the weather. Through the captain, he extended his apologies for missing supper and for his behavior the night before.

Mrs. Hamilton surprised me by not making a fuss. Then I reminded myself that she was not only a lady, but an officer's wife.

"I hope he enjoys a full recovery," she said, giving the Captain a gracious nod. "I sincerely hope he will not be indisposed like that again."

"No, ma'am."

"What about your sergeant? Did he not receive my invitation to join us?"

I felt my feet turn of their own accord towards the nearest door, waiting for an excuse to flee.

"Master Sergeant Johnston has other duties to attend to this evening, ma'am. Perhaps another time."

"I hope so, Captain. He's been kind to our Maggie and I'd like to show our appreciation."

"Of course you would."

Fainting might be a good way of getting out of supper. Too bad I wasn't the kind of girl that fainted. I was the kind that held the smelling salts. Papa raised us to be smart. Mama raised us to be practical.

"I hope you aren't too disappointed, Miss Becker."

I couldn't tell if he was serious or teasing me in punishment.

"I hear you're interested in riding lessons," Carver said.

"Really, Maggie?" Mrs. Hamilton asked. Her tone suggested I should deny any interest immediately.

"My well-meaning, but foolish master sergeant wanted to take Miss Becker riding," Captain Stone said. "Before he tries again, Carver has offered to give her a couple of lessons. He has a couple of younger siblings that he taught to ride. Miss Becker will be in excellent hands."

"Well, in that case, I consent," Mrs. Hamilton said.

"*Gott hilf mir*," I muttered.

"What was that Maggie?"

"Thank you, ma'am."

Either because she was angry at me, or she thought I would question her further, Patience avoided me for the rest of the evening and the next morning. By the time I had supervised breakfast and organized the menus for the day, she had left the house.

"Is Thaddeus back?" I asked Mammy.

"Just back. He came in before dawn. Says he's got a couple of bucks. One for the big dinner. One for the smokehouse. Got a brace of turkeys, too. We'll cook a couple of them tomorrow and make turkey pies. We'll have to save one for Christmas, of course."

I looked toward the back stairs. It wasn't fair of me to bother him so soon. In any case, I wasn't given the chance. A trooper stuck his head in the back door and announced that I had a riding lesson this morning and please dress appropriately.

"I have just the thing," Mammy said, pushing herself out of her chair.

I followed her up to the attic and into the lumber room. In a curtained off corner, I could hear Thaddeus snoring. In addition to old chairs, ugly paintings and thread-bare rugs, there were several trunks. Mammy went to one after the other, opening them up until she found what she was looking for.

"These belonged to old Mrs. Hamilton," she whispered.

"Not Patience's mother?"

"No. Her grandmother." She gave a breathy chuckle. "You wouldn't fit into Madame's clothes, Miss Maggie. You got too much figure."

I'd fit into grandma's clothes instead. How nice.

The clothes were packed between layers of paper and were redolent of lavender. The floral patterns on the muslin dresses were bigger than was fashionable now. The sleeves were fuller. The skirts less full. The materials were gorgeous. Old Mrs. Hamilton must have been closer to my coloring for her choice of hues were exactly what I would have chosen myself. One sapphire blue gown particularly drew my eye. It was high-necked and long-sleeved with a half skirt of shiny black satin that parted at the front like drapes at a window.

"Here," Mammy whispered, carefully pulling out a bundle of navy blue worsted. She passed it to me. "Come on."

She directed me behind a stack of boxes and told me to take off my dress and crinoline. I could see her logic. If we went to my room, we might run into Mrs. Hamilton. Still, I was uncomfortable changing so close to a sleeping man, even if he was Thaddeus.

Of course, even without my dress and crinoline, I had two layers of clothes on. Three if you counted my corset.

Mammy shook out the blue skirt. It was fuller on one side than the other. She slipped it over my head and laced it up at the waist. Then she helped me into the jacket. It was decorated with black chord on the placket and cuffs and buttoned to the throat.

"Loop the extra bit of skirt over your arm. You don't have proper boots and you should have a hat, but you'll do."

We came out from the boxes. Thaddeus was standing there, in stocking feet and shirt sleeves. He grinned.

"You'll more than do, Miss Maggie. You're as pretty as a picture."

I smiled and felt more confident.

My confidence faltered when I met Captain Stone at the corral.

"Lieutenant Carver sends his apologies, but his commanding officer has given him other duties."

"You're his commanding officer," I said.

"True. This is why I feel that, in fairness, I should fill in as your riding instructor."

The lesson was very businesslike. I was taught how to position myself and my skirt on the side-saddle so I was secure and respectably covered. He led the horse for a little while, until I felt more secure, then instructed me on how to hold the reins and let the horse know where I wanted to go.

At first, he walked beside me, no doubt ready to grab the bridle if the horse or I panicked. Then he mounted his horse and rode beside me.

"Do you feel ready to leave the yard?"

No, I thought. "Yes," I said.

"Where do you want to go?"

I pointed in the direction I knew Patience had come from when she returned yesterday. Captain Stone led the way and my horse knew enough to follow. When we were clear of the buildings and gardens, he pulled back so we were riding side by side.

"You could have come to me in the first place," he said.

I was splitting my attention between staying seated in the saddle and wondering where Patience had been seen so his comment startled me.

"You could have told me you wanted to learn to ride," he clarified.

"I never thought about it much before. But then Miss Patience was going riding with you and..." I trailed off. I had no idea how to finish that sentence without telling the truth about my concerns.

"You thought I'd rather go riding with Miss Patience, so you went to my master sergeant for lessons?"

He thought I was jealous. The nerve!

Now I was in a pickle. I didn't want him to think I was envious of Patience, but it was a neat explanation for suddenly wanting to go riding.

"Were you trying to make me jealous, Miss Becker?"

I turned so sharply to stare at him, my horse must have thought I wanted him to go in that direction. Our legs brushed against each other and I almost fell out of the saddle in surprise.

Captain Stone laughed. "Careful, Miss Becker. Best keep your eyes on the road."

The road was a track that led to the cotton fields. The nearest plots had been converted to food production. Beyond them, you could see where the cotton had been grown and picked. We soon reached the sheds where the cotton was stored. The sheds were open on one side so we could see the burlap wrapped bales stacked to the roof. If we had taken the other road out, we would have seen the drying sheds for the tobacco. That was a secondary crop. As with most of the south, cotton was king at Bellevue.

"Do you think Mrs. Hamilton will trade?"

I looked over at Captain Stone, careful not to pull the reins as I did. "I can't say. She's torn."

"She doesn't want to make trouble."

"Nor do I, Captain. Not over cotton, in any case."

"Over Pickens?"

His expression made me turn away. There was no anger, only sadness and that sadness filled me as well. I turned my attention to the road ahead, the sheds, anything but that pained expression. Up until that evening, I had regarded Captain Stone as a friend. I was friendly with Lieutenant Pickens as well, but not close. Not like Captain Stone.

I knew it wasn't fair of me to expect the captain to turn against his own, but I felt betrayed. Now I also felt that somehow I had betrayed him, too.

"When I went to the master sergeant, he told me that drunkenness was part of the problem, that sober, Lieutenant Pickens could control his melancholy. He helped me understand. I consider him a friend. Just as Lieutenant Pickens is your friend."

"I've always considered Johnston my friend as well as being the best damned master sergeant in the cavalry." He held out his hand to me. "I'd like to think we're friends, too."

"Um, friends, yes. Absolutely. Captain, you'll forgive me if I keep both hands on the reins."

He laughed and I suddenly felt happy. I didn't care about Pickens or Patience or anything but those smiling green eyes gazing at me with affection. I didn't even care that I was practically positive those stored bales were not cotton.

CHAPTER EIGHT

My euphoric spirits lasted until we met Patience and Lieutenant Carver on the way back to the house. Patience wasn't in a good mood. Before she noticed us, her smile was brittle. Whatever she was up to, Carver was in the way. Once she noticed us, she was livid.

"How dare you! Where did you get that outfit? That isn't my mother's is it?"

"I've been reliably informed that I have too much figure for your mother's clothes."

She looked so much like she wanted to hit me, my horse backed up.

"That makes sense," Carver said. "You are a tall, slender woman, Miss Patience. I'm sure your mother was also."

He didn't move quickly enough and felt Patience's crop across his knuckles.

"Enough," Captain Stone said. "Miss Hamilton, please comport yourself like the lady I know you are." He didn't chastise me, but he could have. I had let my temper get away from me again.

We circled around and approached the house from the main drive. Patience was coldly silent while Carver chatted about their delightful ride to Wentworth Place. At the house, the gentlemen dismounted and helped us down. I was grateful. My knees were wobbly.

As Captain Stone lifted me down he whispered, "Want me to stay with you?"

I shook my head. Of course I wanted him to stay, but I needed to talk to Patience.

Not that she gave me the chance. When I started to speak, she held a hand up to silence me. I followed her through the front door and saw Mrs. Hamilton on the stairs. My usually gentle employer was looking very stormy.

"I am very disappointed in you, Maggie. I am sure that outfit does not belong to you."

'Of course not," Patience snapped. "It belonged to my grandmother. Since you gave Maggie permission to learn to ride, I gave her permission to make use of grand-mama's old clothes so she would have something suitable to wear."

Mrs. Hamilton was taken aback. I was stunned.

"The waistline is a bit old fashioned, but the color suits her. I'm going to let her keep it." She turned a tight smile in my direction and beckoned me to follow her upstairs. "Come, Maggie. We should change. I'm sure you have duties to attend."

I bobbed a curtsy as I passed Mrs. Hamilton on the stairs.

"How did your riding lesson go?"

"She's a natural," Patience said, not giving me a chance to answer. "I'm sure she won't require any more lessons."

I kept silent until we were in the nursery. Then I stopped her before she could disappear into her room.

"Don't," she said, almost spitting out the word. "You owe me now."

"I know, but that doesn't change the fact that we need to talk."

"I am not meeting Nathaniel. You have nothing to worry about."

I folded my arms and stared at her. How could she say anything so patently absurd? I had plenty to worry about. One of those worries walked through the door. Mrs. Hamilton had followed us upstairs.

"I think I shall have lunch in the dining room," she announced. "I'd like to have a word with Captain Stone."

I had more than enough to be worried about.

Taking time off in the morning gave me ample reason to excuse myself from lunch. With only a few days left before the ball, we had plenty to do in the kitchen. The plantation bakery would take care of baking bread and slab cakes, but Mammy had the best touch for biscuits and pastry. While she fashioned the crusts and oversaw the preparation of fruit fillings, Labelle created the cream fillings and syrups. My job was to oversee the daily meal preparations so they could be free to turn raw ingredients into edible art.

Long after the family meal, I sat with a cup of ersatz coffee, a cold plate and a list. The list contained the things that needed to be done for the party. The dinner and supper menus were laid out with constituent dishes and timelines for preparation. Mammy, Labelle and I had worked that out together. Added to that were the housekeeping chores. I decided to delegate those to Nate. It would serve him right for being so bossy.

Unwritten, I listed what I had to do to keep Captain Stone, and especially Colonel Redmond, from finding out about the missing cotton.

The first item was to confirm that the cotton was really gone.

Mammy was taking a nap in her rocker. She had it placed by the open hearth where she could stay warm and keep watch over the three turkeys turning on the spit. She could sleep through a thunderstorm, yet wake in an instant if one of the children taking turns working the spit let it stop. I let her be and told Labelle that I was going to forage for coffee makings.

It would have been easier to follow the path, but if I was supposed to be gathering herbs and acorns, I had better come back with some. The walk to the cotton sheds took quite a bit longer than the ride this morning, perhaps longer than it need to have taken. I wasn't in a hurry to be proved right.

I was right. The bales were full of straw.

Now what?

"Miss Maggie?"

I almost jumped out of my skin. "Master Sergeant! You startled me."

Master Sergeant dismounted and walked his horse towards me. I hurried to meet him so he wouldn't come too close to the shed.

"Unusual for you to be out so far from the house."

"Not really. I've been too busy to take walks lately, but I needed some ingredients." I showed him my basket. There were about a pint of acorns on the bottom with a mixture of wild herbs and roots on top. "I am forever seeking ways of stretching our coffee supply."

Chalk, the broad-backed grey that had patiently stood by during my embarrassing incident yesterday, seemed determined to undo me today as well. He pulled at the reins. Straw isn't the best food for horses, but he didn't seem to care. He'd sniffed out fodder and wanted a snack.

The bond between horse and rider must have been very strong, because the master sergeant dropped the reins and let Chalk go.

"Something you want to tell me, Miss Maggie?"

"No," I said, with more honesty than sense. I walked away from the shed. I needed to sit down. There was a cart nearby. That would do. I climbed up the gate and brushed the dirt from my hands.

It was a warm day for December, yet I felt chilled.

"Maybe you should tell me anyway," he suggested.

We sat and I talked.

My guess was that Patience was working with the Wentworth family to get their cotton to market before it was bought up cheap or confiscated by the army. I didn't specify the family but I suggested that Miss Patience would have needed help, but I had no idea to whom she'd turn. I also mentioned that I'd heard rumors of a widow who managed to get her husband's crop to New Orleans, and from there to England.

"I doubt she'd do that, Miss Maggie. It would make more sense to ship it to New York. There's been a fair amount of trade in cotton from the south."

"But we're at war."

He gave a harsh laugh. "Evidently our president feels it's better for the south to get guns from the north than guns and ammunition from Europe."

I shook my head. "Sounds crazy to me. But then war seems crazy to me. If Mr. Lincoln weren't freeing the slaves, I'd see no good in it at all."

I picked at the handle of my basket, nervous about asking my next question. "Will we get into trouble over this?"

"You? Probably not. Especially if you take what you know to Captain Stone." He paused, looking grimmer than his lopsided mouth usually made him look. "The Hamiltons are another thing all together. Captain Stone may be lenient, but I doubt Colonel Redmond will be happy about being strung along."

This was what I'd concluded as well. "Things won't be very comfortable around here for the rest of the winter."

"No."

"So, maybe we should do something about it."

Master Sergeant insisted on walking me back to the house. We had ironed out a plan long before we reached the yard, but he thought that it would look as though we were skulking around if he didn't accompany me to the back door. At the bottom of the steps, he bowed low over my hand and gave me a wink. This gave the kitchen staff too much to talk about, so I retired to my room, claiming a headache.

My head did in fact ache and I was unbelievably tired. I fell asleep and woke to a dark room. Panicked, I pulled a skirt and blouse on over my underdress, forgetting about the crinoline that should have gone in between. In the nursery, Mammy was sitting by the fire. The clock on the mantle told me it was past midnight.

"I brought you up a bowl of soup, Miss Maggie. It's just there on the hearth. It's all that worrying about people that's made you tuckered out. That's what I told Mrs. Hamilton when she asked about you."

I bent over and gave her cheek a kiss. Her skin was leathery, but soft like a chammy. She gave my chin a pinch, then hefted herself out of the chair.

"You sit here, Miss Maggie. It's time I found my bed."

I sat and imagined the children Mammy had comforted in this chair. In some ways I was just another one in the long line.

"Oh, one other thing," Mammy said, keeping her voice low. "Captain Stone left something for you in the kitchen. Said it was particularly for you." She grinned as I started to stand. "Don't you worry. It can wait to tomorrow."

I wondered if she tormented her other children, too.

CHAPTER NINE

Coffee.

A full pound bag of green beans waited for me on the kitchen table. Under the burlap bag was a note: "Not to be saved for Christmas."

While the half-and-half blend I made for the officers brewed, I roasted a quarter of the beans. When Captain Stone arrived for his midmorning coffee, the fresh-roasted, fresh-ground coffee was almost ready.

"Thank you," I said, as soon as he was seated at the table. Several turkey pies were cooling at one end, but there was room enough for our cups and a plate of broken molasses curls.

"My pleasure," he said, helping himself to a wafer thin shard. "I thought you'd appreciate coffee more than flowers. Mm. These taste better than they look."

"The intact curls will be filled with brandy cream for the ball. They're very delicate. We are benefitting from the breakages." I brought the coffee pot over. "Why would you bring me flowers?"

He gave me a playful smile. "I didn't. I brought you coffee. Would you have preferred flowers?"

"No. But..."

"Why does a man bring a woman a gift?"

I felt the heat of a blush suffuse my face and tried to hide dipping my head and concentrating on pouring the coffee.

"I know I disappointed you in how I dealt with Pickens," he said, serious now.

"How is Lieutenant Pickens? Is he feeling better?"

"He was at supper last night. He thought you were avoiding him. I told him you would have had to have been aware he'd be there to do that."

"True."

"Would you have avoided him?"

"No!" Embarrassed, I had been avoiding his gaze. Now I met him, eye to eye. "But I would have been uncomfortable. That's the plain truth. I'm sorry if that disappoints you."

He shook his head, lips curving up in a smile. I watched the smile reach his eyes, then concentrated on my coffee lest I be caught staring. Once again, I was suffused with happiness. Then I remembered my predicament.

"Is something wrong, Miss Becker?"

I smiled. It wasn't too difficult while drinking wonderful coffee across from such a handsome and thoughtful man. If only I could confide in him. I couldn't. It was bad enough I had brought the master sergeant into this mess. I couldn't risk the captain's career as well.

"I'm fine, Captain. I'm just a little worn down with all the preparations. I'll make sure I'm at supper tonight, though. We don't want Lieutenant Pickens thinking I'm unforgiving."

Despite what I told Captain Stone, I was not at all worn down. My long sleep the day before had restored my energy and the gift of coffee had restored my spirits. In fact, knowing that the coffee was given, not merely in gratitude for my efforts, or in friendship, put me in a wonderful mood. I even started to believe Master Sergeant and I would be able to avert disaster.

My mood buoyed me through the awkwardness of meeting Lieutenant Pickens at supper. It took the edge off of Mrs. Hamilton's comments about the master sergeant, even when Patience joined in with the teasing. It saw me through an intensely busy day as everything was turned upside-down when Mrs. Hamilton took an interest in the ball preparations and Christmas decorations on this last day before the event. My good mood wasn't impervious, however.

While Junie and one of the other girls helped Mrs. Hamilton dress for dinner, I went over the final checklist for the next day.

"You've done very well, my dear," Mrs. Hamilton said. "Make sure the kitchen table is clear after supper is served so the musicians can have their meal. I'm counting on you to preside over them as well as make sure everything runs smoothly."

"Yes, ma'am."

I should have guessed. I wasn't going to the ball.

Roasting coffee beans was a delicate operation. It had to be done in small batches, always keeping the beans moving. The difference between a perfectly roasted bean and a burnt one could be a matter of seconds. I discovered I had a nose for the job. I could tell by aroma just the right moment to put the beans aside to cool and start a new batch. More than that, I could control the depth of the roast which would make the difference between a coffee drunk by the cupful in the morning and the dark nutty drink poured into demitasse after supper.

It was something I could control. Maybe the only thing I could control.

"Miss Maggie! Miss Maggie!" Junie came running into the kitchen with Mrs. Hamilton's ball gown trailing behind.

"Shush," Mammy said. "Now is not the time, child. Come tell me what the matter is."

"I done burned Mrs. Hamilton's gown with the iron. She's gonna be so mad at me."

I smiled. In part it was because of Junie's grammar failing under pressure. Mrs. Hamilton was trying to improve the girl's language skills. I have to admit, I was also vindictively pleased that the gown was burned.

"How bad is it?" I asked.

"You keep your mind on your roasting, Miss Maggie. Junie, you take the gown to Mama Lou. She used to take care of the first Mrs. Hamilton's clothes and she'll know better than anyone how to repair the damage."

Mammy waited until Junie was gone and I was finished my current batch of beans. Then she took me to task for unchristian thoughts.

"Because there is no denying, I know what was crossing your mind then." She patted me on the shoulder. "Things will work out better than you think. Now, do you have coffee brewed, or just a pile of beans?"

"I've got coffee made."

"Good. Cause you're about to have company."

I didn't know how she did it, but she always knew when Captain Stone was about to enter. When he did, my day improved immeasurably.

"Do you have time for coffee?" he asked. "I imagine you'll have things to do to get yourself ready for this evening. I expect you ladies will be having your lunch upstairs while you prepare or rest up or whatever you do."

I laughed. "Mrs. Hamilton will have a nap. I'm not sure what Miss Patience will do before she dresses for tonight."

"And you?"

"I'll freshen up and put on a clean gown, but I don't have to dress up for this evening." I turned to fetch the coffee pot and hide my disappointment.

He grasped my arm.

"You're not dressing up for the evening?"

"Mrs. Hamilton wants me to make sure things go smoothly." I laid a hand on his arm. "It's all right. It's not like I have a ball gown or anything. Besides, I will be too busy with things. Getting dressed up and doing my hair and such will take too much time."

Captain Stone looked down at me. He didn't look pleased and I hoped I wasn't the object of his wrath. His eyes softened and I was reassured. Soon enough he might be legitimately angry at me. I didn't want him to be mad at me for this.

"I better let you get back to work," he said. "You will be joining the dinner party, if nothing else. I'll make sure of it."

I needed to meet with the master sergeant about this evening. Our plan was simple. Fireworks were planned. When they went off, he was going to make sure the cotton shed "accidently" caught fire. I had a butternut shirt for him to wear over his uniform so if anyone saw him, they would assume Confederate sabotage.

Master Sergeant Johnston would not have achieved his rank if he had not been very capable. It was easier to become an officer than a top non-com. Still, if I could have seen my way clear, I would have preferred to have had Thaddeus do the deed. He had offered, despite the risk. I was worried that Thaddeus would be a prime suspect if the question of arson came up.

In any case, Thaddeus was needed to serve as butler. Nate was very good, but we could hardly have him serving his family and neighbors. Instead, he was going to be in charge of taking food and drink to the soldiers who would be having their own party at the stables. If anyone asked for the master sergeant, he was to announce that he saw him somewhere else. One of the benefits of me not attending the ball was that I would be another person who could cover for the master sergeant.

Now I wasn't sure what I'd be doing.

I was just getting my wrapper on when Junie came running down the back stairs calling for me. Again.

"Mrs. Hamilton wants you now, Miss Maggie. Right now."

I sighed, hung my wrapper on the hook beside the back door, and followed her up.

Evidently, Captain Stone worked fast. Mrs. Hamilton was in something between a tizzy and a snit about his demand that I be included in the dinner party.

"He seems to think Colonel Redmond will expect your presence. I cannot see why."

"Because she was at dinner the last time," Patience said, while re-stringing a strand of beads. "I keep telling you, you can't raise Maggie up to being a companion one moment and turn her into a housekeeper the next, even if she does the work of one. People don't understand."

"How was I to know that you would suggest a ball?" Mrs. Hamilton shook her finger at her stepdaughter. "Formal dinners are one thing, but suggesting a ball when your father is a prisoner of war is unseemly. I could not have anticipated this turn of events."

Patience shrugged.

"Don't shrug at me, miss. Tell me what Maggie is going to wear that will be suitable for this evening and her station. Tell me." She waved a hand in triumph. "You can't, can you."

"You're wrong, Step-mama." Patience knotted her strand and held the loop of crystal beads up to the firelight. "I anticipated this problem and gave Mama Lou a dress to adjust to Maggie's figure." She handed me the beaded necklace. "I feel like a fairy godmother. It's rather fun."

CHAPTER TEN

I did not stay upstairs to do my feminine preparations with the other ladies of the house. I beat a hasty retreat and lunched with Mammy in the kitchen before putting the final dinner preparations in motion and taking a walk around the house to see that everything was in order.

Boughs of holly and evergreen wound around the bannisters and were draped over lintels. More elaborate arrangements, with imported blown glass ornaments, decorated the mantles.

The summer parlor had been cleared of bulky furniture for dancing. A few chairs and benches lined the walls for people to sit between dances.

The family parlor was crowded with extra chairs and a couple of card tables for the people who preferred gambling over dancing.

All the leaves were in the dining table. Nate was supervising the setting, his final task before leaving the house. Thaddeus was setting up the bar.

"I hear you'll be coming to the dance after all, Miss Maggie. Sure is a funny situation."

It sure was.

Labelle came to tell me that Mama Lou was expecting me. With a last glance around, I hurried out.

I wasn't expecting to stay away long. I thought Mama Lou would have me try on the gown and I'd go back to the house to greet the early arrivals. I thought I might even have a chance to check in with the master sergeant.

This was not Mama Lou's plan.

She had a bath set up in the bakery. Everything that was going to be baked was already baked and delivered so we had the toasty-warm place to ourselves.

"Before you argue with me, *cheri*, remember that you have been working hard and long for days now and no *bon homme* is going to ask you to dance unless you wash the kitchen smell off you."

"No one's going to ask me to dance at all."

"Feh!"

She showed me the dress.

I recognized it from the trunk. It was the sapphire blue gown, but less of it. The bodice was lower, the sleeves shorter. The black half skirt was gone. Spangled gauze took its place. The crystal bead necklace was the perfect accessory.

My eyes welled up with tears. I felt like Cinderella. Blindly, I allowed my second fairy godmother to undress me and lead me to the bath.

My third fairy godmother turned out to be Lieutenant Carver. Since I couldn't very well show up at the ball in a coach, he acted as my escort across the yard. He wrapped me in his overcoat and lifted me across the stretch of half-frozen mud at the bottom of the kitchen stairs. He retrieved his coat once we were inside, then walked back out and around the house to enter through the front door.

"Oh, Miss Maggie," Labelle said, looking up from her gravy. "You are *trés belle*, as my mama would say. *Trés belle* indeed."

"Pretty as a picture," Mammy agreed. "Now get up those stairs so you can make your entrance. Mrs. Hamilton is wondering what happened to you."

Going up the back stairs with a full hoop was challenging. I had to take a moment to make sure everything was still where it was supposed to be. Then I had to get up my courage to descend the main stairs.

I listened at the top. Colonel Redmond had arrived. His voice carried, as did Mrs. Hamilton's. I heard them greet Lieutenant Carver and decided I'd better get down there before he was sent out to find me again.

"There you are, Maggie. Right on time."

Patience startled me. She looked lovelier than usual in her ruby red gown. I only wished Nate could see her. She looped her arm through mine and for a moment she reminded me of Matty as she dragged me off for our grand entrance. Matty was always the brave one when it came to new situations. I'd shy away from putting myself forward and she'd nudge me along. Tonight Patience was doing the nudging and I was very grateful.

By the time we reached the landing, the band started playing. The fanfare drew attention to us. At first the looks were purely appreciative. Then the people who recognized me started to look puzzled. Much to my surprise, Mrs. Hamilton was not at all upset. She didn't seem to notice that Captain Stone was gazing at me with appreciation. She just gave me a knowing smile and nodded slightly in the direction of the ballroom.

Looking very dapper in his dress uniform was Master Sergeant Johnston. I almost fainted. And the band played on.

Dinner was a blur.

Master Sergeant led me into the dining room and sat beside me. My usual escort, Lieutenant Pickens was absent. Perhaps Mrs. Hamilton bumped him off the guest list to make room for my supposed beau.

Colonel Redmond had been given the head of the table as ranking officer. Table talk between the two ends wasn't possible, which was a mercy.

I was close enough to Mrs. Hamilton to hear her speculating with Mr. and Mrs. Wentworth about Patience and Captain Stone. I only hoped they didn't know their son was her stepdaughter's real suitor. She also asked Master Sergeant a few embarrassing questions about his prospects after the war.

At the other end of the table, Patience was avoiding Colonel Redmond's inquiries about the cotton.

After dinner, the military band went to join their fellow troopers and the musicians from town tuned up for the dance.

Captain Stone led Mrs. Redmond onto the floor for the first dance. It turned out Master Sergeant was not a dancer. For the second piece, the captain invited Mrs. Hamilton, but she deferred to Patience, saying that she needed to rest after dancing with the colonel.

Lieutenant Carver asked me to dance. From then on, there was always an officer at hand to lead me to the floor. In contrast, the plantation gentlemen and their ladies were cool towards me. I was beginning to think that Mrs. Hamilton had been right that I had no place at this kind of function. Then Captain Stone asked me to stand up with him for a slow waltz.

"What do you think about my tactics, Miss Becker?"

"Your tactics?"

"I ordered Master Sergeant Johnston to attend to take the heat off you with Mrs. Hamilton. I know she still harbors hopes that I will become smitten with her stepdaughter. It would be very awkward for you if she knew I was completely, and irretrievably smitten with you."

"Oh."

It wasn't the brightest of comments but I was torn between being elated and irritated. I was very happy to hear that he cared for me. Although his tone of voice was playful, his eyes spoke to the depth of his feelings. Yet, I could have wished that his tactics hadn't interfered with my plans. I needed the master sergeant elsewhere.

We glided around the room and I set aside my worries to enjoy the feeling of Captain Stone's hand on my waist. The width of my skirt kept us at close to arm's length, making me wonder who came up with this crazy fashion. Yet, even as that thought crossed my mind, I gazed up into the captain's intense green eyes and lost myself in the warmth of their expression.

As far as I was concerned, the dance could have lasted forever. I could have danced all night. Too soon, the music ended and the musicians took a break. Colonel Redmond required Captain Stone's attention. Then Patience demanded mine.

"Let's freshen up," she said. She looped her arm in mine and leaned in toward me. "Nathaniel told me what you are planning. We need to talk."

She led me upstairs. As soon as we were alone, she started speaking in a rushed whisper.

"You can't set fire to the straw. It won't burn the same as cotton."

"Will anyone else know that? Anyone who hasn't also sold their cotton to New York mills?"

"How did you know?"

I didn't answer that question. I didn't know for certain that the Wentworth crop was involved, let alone any of the other plantations. It was a lucky guess. "Have all of them moved all their cotton?"

She shook her head. "Some haven't gotten involved at all. Some are only moving part of their crop and claiming a poor year. Mr. Wentworth already sold his cotton before the army got involved. He transported ours with his."

"*Mein gott!* Why not say you sold our cotton, too? Why this crazy subterfuge?"

"Because we hadn't sold our cotton and without father, I had no idea how to sell our cotton."

"Then why not sell to the army if you're sending the crop to northern mills?"

"Gold," Patience said simply. "We're getting paid in gold. If we sold to the army's suppliers, we'd get script and who knows what that will be worth in a year."

"Let's hope we don't have to spend it on staying out of prison. When did Nate tell you?"

"While you were dancing with the captain. He was trying to get a message to you about taking the master sergeant's place."

"No!"

Suddenly my simple plan seemed nightmarishly complicated and incredibly stupid.

"That's what I said, too," Patience said. "Whatever we do, he can't be a part of it."

On our way back downstairs, we met Junie running up.

"Miss Maggie! Miss Maggie!"

"Junie, will you please stop running around yelling my name. It's getting tiresome. I'm sure Mrs. Hamilton doesn't appreciate it either."

The girl looked crestfallen. "It's Mrs. Hamilton," she said in a more subdued voice. "She's fainted dead away."

Patience and I picked up our skirts and ran down the steps.

"Where is my stepmother?" Patience demanded.

"This way Miss Patience," Carver said, indicating the parlor. "We placed her on a settee, as best we could. Miss Maggie, Colonel Redmond and the captain want to see you in the office."

"In just a moment," I said, following Patience.

With the heat of all the extra people and the clouds of cigar smoke in the air, the room was oppressively stuffy.

"Open a window, Thaddeus. Junie, go fetch Mrs. Hamilton's shawl so she doesn't catch a chill." I reached into my pocket and pulled out a vial of smelling salts.

"Hold on to it," Patience said. "I have mine. Go find out what the captain wants and shoo some of these folks out with you."

"I'll do the shooing," Carver said. "You better get to the office."

"Has anyone died?" I asked.

"Not yet."

"Then maybe you could get the musicians to strike up a dance, something to distract people."

"Yes, ma'am."

Master Sergeant was at the door to the office. He was looking more worried than grim. That didn't auger well.

"Am I in trouble?"

"Can't say, Miss Maggie."

He gave two sharp raps on the door and then opened it for me.

Colonel Redmond was sitting at the massive oak desk. I hadn't been in the office since Captain Stone had taken it over. I felt a surge of territorial imperative. Redmond didn't belong at Major Hamilton's desk. Captain Stone didn't look any happier. He was standing stiffly at attention to the right. To the left, two guards bracketed Nate.

I gripped my smelling salts, like a talisman. I might need them yet.

Colonel Redmond stood and addressed me. "Miss Becker, were you aware that you had a Confederate officer on the property, masquerading as a slave?"

"Of course," I said, quite steadily, I thought. "Nathaniel Wentworth was one of our patients. He wasn't well enough to leave with the Confederate evacuation. He gave us his parole and went to work as soon as he was able."

Redmond nodded. "That's what Captain Stone reported. I was worried he was trying to protect you."

I stifled a sigh of relief.

"One thing, Miss Becker. Why didn't Wentworth seek asylum with his family? Why hide here until one of your neighbors saw him and gave him away?"

Captain Stone interjected. "Miss Becker was probably not aware that, with the exception of senior officers, we have a policy of accepting a wounded soldier's parole."

Redmond gave the captain a wry look. "You were aware of that policy, Captain. You could have told her."

I dropped the vial of smelling salts back into my pocket. Fainting was not a problem. Fear was keeping my wits sharp. I didn't need *sal volotile*.

Nate pulled away from his guards. "It's all my fault. Maggie, that is Miss Becker, was protecting me."

He was going to fall on his sword. I couldn't allow that. Patience would kill me.

"He's right," I said, cutting in. "It is Nate's fault."

Nate and his guards stared at me in shock. Colonel Redmond was obviously surprised. Captain Stone...well I decided I had better not look for his reaction in case it undermined my resolve.

"Nate, that is Mr. Wentworth, should have gone home to his family but he was concerned about the Union Army coming to Bellevue. He stayed for Miss Hamilton's sake and I hid him among the slaves for her sake as well. Captain Stone has been going along with our folly because he is truly a gentleman."

I held my breath while Colonel Redmond considered my words.

"Your parole is given, Wentworth?"

Nate bowed. "My politics have not changed, sir. I still believe that each state has the right to determine their course with minimal federal interference. However, my perspective on slavery has changed considerably. I will not fight to maintain that institution."

Redmond shook his head. "Yes, but does that mean your parole is given?"

"Yes, sir."

"Very well. Do you think, Miss Becker, that suitable garments can be found for Mr. Wentworth so he can join his family at the party?"

I shrugged. "I think Thaddeus might be able to solve that problem."

"Fine. Go take care of that. Not you, Miss Becker. Stone, pull up a chair for the lady."

He carried two straight-back chairs and placed them in front of the desk. I had to perch at the edge to accommodate my skirt. Never again would I look at the ladies in these gowns with envy.

As soon as the colonel was seated, the captain sat beside me.

"You were right, Seth, Miss Becker was the right person to deal with this mess. You should arrange to marry the lady before the end of winter. By next Christmas, you could be a full colonel."

Captain Stone took my hand in his. "With the colonel's permission, I fully intend to propose this evening. Since I will have to ask Mrs. Hamilton's permission as well, I thought I'd wait until Wentworth and Miss Patience are sorted out. That will give me a tactical advantage with the lady." He twisted around so he could cup my hand in both of his. "Would that be all right with you, Maggie?"

I decided to forgive him and his commander for speaking about me as if I wasn't in the room.

"Yes, Seth." I grinned. "That would be a sound strategy."

CHAPTER ELEVEN

As soon as she saw me, Mrs. Hamilton told me to have supper set forward and to have coffee and tea brought out immediately. Tea, she explained loudly and repeatedly, would set her to rights.

Patience followed me to the kitchen to get a report. She knew that Nate had been arrested and wanted assurance that he was not about to be summarily shot. There was too much going on to do more than reassure her Nate was safe. I would have liked to have said that all was well, but I wasn't sure about that yet.

"We got everything under control," Mammy said. "You better get back to the party before you're fetched."

Sure enough, Seth was on his way to the kitchen. We met in the side hall outside of the office. He took a quick look around and pulled me into the now empty room, shutting the door behind us.

He clasped both of my hands in his. "I'll do this formally later, but do you really want to marry me or did Colonel Redmond pressure you into it?"

"I could ask you the same thing."

He shook his head impatiently. "You know I love you."

I tilted my chin up and to the side so I could make eye contact.

"No. You said you were smitten with me. You could get over being smitten. My brother has been smitten with and gotten over at least three girls since he was nine years old." I smiled up into those gorgeous green eyes. "If it will help, I'll tell you that I'm quite sure I love you."

It must have helped because the next thing I knew, his arms were around me and I was being lifted and pulled into a close embrace, hoop tilted out behind me like a bell being rung. I probably looked ridiculous. I didn't let that stop me from enjoying the heavenly sensation of being thoroughly kissed.

We rejoined the party in time for Nate's entrance. If anyone wondered why he suddenly appeared, he didn't give them a chance to ask.

"Ladies and gentlemen, I am very pleased to be back among family and friends, old and new. On this evening, eighteen hundred and sixty-two years ago, Jesus Christ our Lord was born in a manger to bring us peace and salvation. What better time for me to turn to the woman who brought me peace and salvation in body and spirit."

He took Patience's hand and drew her to towards him.

"Miss Hamilton, Patience, will you do me the honor of accepting my hand in marriage?"

She smiled, no, glowed up at him.

"My father told me I should say yes if you should ask. So yes, my love. I would be happy to marry you."

Patience was immediately taken into the arms of her future mother-in-law. Nate shook hands with his father and accepted the congratulations of his neighbors, then turned to his future mother-in-law for her blessing. She really didn't have much choice in the matter. It was a tactical victory.

Seth saved Mrs. Hamilton from having to deal with the Wentworths by inviting the guests to look out the windows in the ballroom. "Or if you don't mind the cold, come out to the porch for a better view. My quartermaster has a background in munitions and has arranged a display of fireworks."

I was feeling a little overheated, so a little cold air was welcome. Besides, that was where Seth was going. He walked to the end of the porch and waved his saber.

Moments later, a red white and blue star-burst exploded overhead. Next, there was a rocket that buzzed high over the fields and showered down green light, followed by shorter bursts of white sparkling against the green like lights on a tree. When the sky had cleared, another rocket went off and there was a much larger explosion closer to the ground.

"Oops," Seth said. "There goes the cotton. Merry Christmas."

The fire was still burning when the last guest left. It was like a second sunset on the horizon.

Mrs. Hamilton had gone to bed as soon as she could excuse herself. Patience had followed as soon as it was clear that Nate was going home with his parents. I was waiting, playing *Stille Nacht* on the piano because, as my Papa often used to point out, I was born with a strong sense of irony.

Seth walked in, smelling of smoke and trailed by Lieutenants Carver and Osmund.

"Where's Lieutenant Pickens?" I asked. "Is he all right?"

"He's fine," Seth said. "He and the master sergeant are keeping an eye on the fire while it burns itself out. Colonel Redmond isn't happy with him, but it was an accident after all."

"Right," Carver said. "An accident. I think poor Pickens just missed blowing things up. Did it in the mines before he turned to law. I bet blowing things up, as opposed to blowing people up, is quite satisfying for him." He flopped down in a chair. "Pour us a whisky, will you Clive? I've got to wash the taste of ash and smoke out of my throat. Better still, grab the bottle and we'll take it up with us.

"Sound decision," Seth said. "Just let me pour a couple of shots before you go." He brought me a glass and sat down on the bench beside me. The clock began to chime midnight. "Merry Christmas," he toasted.

Feeling rather bold, I took my taste of whisky from his lips. It was so good, I went back for seconds.

"Do you think Mrs. Hamilton will let me propose officially at breakfast?"

I grinned. "Give her until supper and she'll think it was her idea all along."

Softly I played the lead in and sang.

"We wish you a Merry Christmas
We wish you a Merry Christmas
We wish you a Merry Christmas
And a peaceful...and loving...and Happy New Year."

~ * ~

If you enjoyed this book, please consider writing a short review and posting it on Amazon, Goodreads and/or Barnes and Noble. Reviews are very helpful to other readers and are greatly appreciated by authors, especially me. When you post a review, drop me an email and let me know and I may feature part of it on my blog/site. Thank you. ~ Alison

writer@alisonbruce.ca

MATTY

By Kat Flannery

My Dearest Mag,

Much has happened since I last saw you. After you left Fort Leavenworth, General Worthington was ordered to volunteer at Camp Douglas in Illinois. We travelled by train, a most horrendous experience due to my motion sickness, and Mrs. Worthington was not happy to see me waylaid for the entire trip. In between bouts of illness, Abigail, much to her mother's disapproval, read me Tamerlane and Other Poems, by Edgar Allan Poe. You know the one, it was Pa's favorite. Mr. Poe is remarkable, Mag, a real gem. I almost love him as much as Shakespeare. His words are that of a genius, and when I read them I can feel Pa around me.

I was not prepared for the sight that greeted us upon entering the Camp. It held no similarities to Fort Leavenworth. It was dreadful. I did not feel safe on my own and because I was not allotted a chaperone, I rarely left the cabin. I was relieved when Mrs. Worthington shuffled us off to a town house in Chicago a few weeks later. Tomorrow we leave for Fort Wayne where the General will oversee the training of soldiers for the coming war. I am nervous about the journey, but at the same time I am relieved to be distancing myself from the hostilities here.

Abigail and I have become fast friends, when Mrs. Worthington allows it. The Madame is not fond of me, and is quite adamant that her daughter set her sights on other girls for friendship. Without Abigail's companionship, I'd surely go mad. I miss you more than words could convey.

I only hope Mama and Werner stay safe during this time, as do you, dear sister. I pray that I see you one day soon, but I fear my request will not be fulfilled until the war has ended.

God be with you always.

Your loving sister,
Matty

CHAPTER ONE

Fort Wayne, Michigan
December 1862

What had she done? Matty Becker was going to hell, and there'd be no one to save her. A loud snore echoed from the other room. She peeked around the corner and caught a glimpse of Colonel Black's stocking feet. She'd burn for sure. She glanced at the paper she held and groaned. She was a horrible, devious, scheming letch. Maggie wouldn't be pleased. *Maggie wasn't here.* Another snore blew into the kitchen and she placed her head onto the table banging her forehead twice. There was no turning back now.

Last night she'd pushed aside her conscience and let fear guide her. For her plan to work, she'd have to throw all sense to the dogs, not that she hadn't done so already by following through with the blasted thing. She couldn't fail now. If her family found out what she'd done they'd never forgive her. Worse yet, if Colonel Black found out she'd be locked behind bars, a fate far better than the one that got her in this mess to begin with.

She placed the paper on the table and went into the bedroom. Colonel Black lay on the bed with his clothes stripped off and tossed about the floor. He'd been out for nine hours and would wake any minute. Matty stood, pushed all thoughts of reason from her mind and removed her dress, corset and pantaloons. Her face heated and the room spun. He rolled over and she jumped into the bed next to him, pretending to sleep. She knew the moment he'd woken. The bed stilled and she couldn't breathe the air was so stiff.

"What the hell?" He sat up and she knew the instant he saw her. "Son of a bitch."

She felt his nudge once, twice and now a shove almost knocking her from the bed.

"Wake the hell up," he growled.

She squeezed her eyes closed and willed strength into her soul so she could face the dark Colonel. She rolled over pretending to wipe the sleep from her eyes.

"Who are you?" He placed his head in his hands. She'd bet he had one heck of a headache.

"Your wife," she said.

"The hell you are." He shot out of bed without grabbing the sheet, and she averted her eyes.

"Please cover yourself." She held up the sheet and he ripped it from her hand. "The marriage license is in the kitchen on the table if you do not believe me."

She watched as he grabbed his head and closed his eyes. The heavy dose of laudanum she'd placed in his drink the night before had done the trick and it wasn't but a mere suggestion they marry that the Colonel jumped to the challenge. Soon they were standing in the dining room in front of a preacher. Words were spoken—words she thought to say with someone she loved, someone who'd wanted her. Her stomach lurched and her mouth watered with the urge to vomit.

"How did this happen?" he asked sitting on the end of the bed.

"Mrs. Worthington sent me to see if you needed anything."

"I was drinking." He looked at her. "I was drunk."

She shrugged.

He stood holding the sheet tight to his midsection.

She couldn't help but notice the rippled stomach and defined muscles on his chest.

"We can annul. I had too much to drink. My head wasn't clear."

She shook her head.

He frowned.

"We have consummated." A lie of course but she was desperate.

His mouth fell open. A moment she knew he'd not remember. After the preacher left, she'd taken him to the bedroom where he passed out before hitting the bed.

"Impossible. I'd remember that."

She shook her head again praying he'd buy the fib.

He pulled on his pants and dress shirt. "I don't even know you. Why in hell would I marry you?"

"My name is Matty Beck—Black. I was employed with the Worthington's. You've come to dinner several times."

His brown eyes lit with recognition. "You're the house maid."

"Yes."

"I married a maid?"

The words stung and she turned from him so he wouldn't see the disappointment upon her face.

"Why would you marry me if I was into the spirits?"

"You seemed fine to me."

He took a step toward her. "Why would you marry me at all when you don't even know me?"

She gripped the blanket on the bed. "You...you said kind words, and I...I believed them."

"How desperate are you to marry a stranger?" he yelled. "You found out who my father is. You want money. You tricked me."

Well, he got the last one right, but the first two irritated her. She was not the kind of person to marry for money. Really, who did he think she was?

"Sorry to disappoint you but I refused my inheritance years ago."

"If you mean to say that I could not find myself a suitable husband because I am a maid, then you're wrong."

"That is exactly what I am saying Miss—"

"Black."

"The hell it is."

He went into the kitchen picked up the marriage license and stared at it.

Matty dressed quickly and inched into the room. Confusion pulled at his features and she began to feel sorry for him. This was her fault. She'd planned this. Now she had to continue telling the lie she'd told. She glanced outside and shivered. *Boldness, be my tongue.* Shakespeare's words echoed in her mind. It was worth it. She'd been living in fear for a week. Colonel Black had been her saviour, and she risked a life full of love and happiness for this—a lie in which she'd speak for the rest of her life. She swallowed back the lump in her throat and willed the tears not to fall.

"Why can't I remember?" He glanced at her. "And why in hell would I marry you?"

She glared at him.

"A serving girl."

"You asked me, remember?"

"No, damn it, I do not remember!"

She searched through his cupboards until she found the coffee. "How do you like your coffee?"

"Strong." He slumped into a chair. His shirt, still unbuttoned, showed the taut skin beneath and his brown hair lay messed falling around his face. The frown, a permanent fixture, creased his forehead.

The water boiled and the grounds steeped to the top of the pot. The smell of coffee filled the room, and she inhaled a calming breath.

"You don't look the least bit upset over this."

She placed a cup in front of him before sitting in the other chair. "Believe only half of what you see and nothing of what you hear."

He raised a brow.

"Edgar Allan Poe, one of my favorite authors."

He rolled his eyes.

"Last night, you seemed fine to me."

"Yes, I suppose when I'm the one who can't remember a bloody thing." He took a sip. "If it's money you want, I'll give it. Just tell me how much."

A sharp pain shot across her chest and remorse settled heavy in her stomach.

"I do not want your money," she whispered.

"Of course you do, why else would you marry me."

For protection. She shrugged.

"How much do you want?"

Taken aback at his harsh and very predictable words, she sat straight in the chair. "I told you I do not want your money."

"Look, Miss—"

"Black."

"No," he growled and his face contorted into hard lines.

"Yes." She picked up the license. "The paper says so."

He ripped it from her. "This is a forgery."

"How so?" She needed him to believe her—to at least try and stay married until she could come up with another plan.

"This is not my signature." He pushed the paper into her face.

"It most certainly is."

He shook his head and she watched as his dark curls fell into his eyes.

Unable to utter another lie, she stood. "I must go to the Worthington's and collect my things." The hair on her neck pricked and she flexed her hands.

He pushed from the table and buttoned his shirt before reaching behind the chair to grab his cane.

"The hell you are. I am getting to the bottom of this before you go anywhere."

She nodded.

"I plan on stopping by the preacher's, and if I find out that this is some sort of Tom Foolery I will press charges."

"You will see I speak the truth." *Liar, liar, liar.* She bit her tongue to keep from confessing.

"We shall see."

Give thy thoughts no tongue. She grabbed her scarf and wrapped it around her neck so that it hid the moth holes. She pulled out the wool mittens mother had sent from her pockets and put them on.

"Must you take so long?" he yelled and banged the end of the cane onto the hardwood floor.

The weather hadn't done the cane much good. The wood was faded and splintered.

"What is it you are staring at?"

"Excuse me?"

"Have you never seen a cane before?" He stomped the butt end of the stick onto the wooden floor again.

"Why, of course."

"Then what the hell is so fascinating about mine?" He leaned in and she smelled the hint of brandy from last night.

"It is cracked." She pointed.

He brought the cane close and squinted. Did he need spectacles? How had he not known it was split? She'd bet it was from all the banging he'd done with it.

"I know someone who could make you another one."

He glared and slammed the cane down.

She jumped.

"Do you always interfere in other people's business, Matty?"

"No, I only thought—"

"You thought what? That I'd be grateful for the suggestion? That I'd smile graciously and offer my thanks? Not after the night I've had, and definitely not after you've tricked me so."

"I was merely being helpful. That is all."

"I do not need your help nor do I want it. And I don't need a bloody wife." He leaned in and growled, "So next time you feel the need to extend your kindness, keep it to yourself."

Her brown eyes flashed with fury.

"Love all, trust few, do wrong to none," she whispered.

"What? What did you say?"

"It is William Shakespeare, Sir, and it was one of my father's favorite sayings. It is also a reminder to be kind to others."

"How—"

"How would a lowly maid know of Edgar Allan Poe and William Shakespeare? My father was a school master and educated his daughters and son." She met his stare with one of her own.

He clamped his mouth shut, speechless for the first time since he woke.

Thank goodness.

"Shall we go, dear Sir, and see if I am a conspirator to such things as forgery?" She tipped her chin and walked out into the cold.

Cole drove away from Preacher Ryan's home stunned at what he'd heard. Matty had told the truth. They were in fact married. He pushed his chin into the scarf wrapped around his neck and peeked at her sitting beside him in the carriage. Snow had begun to fall in thick white flakes clinging to her lashes and cheeks. He hadn't thought to put the canvas cover over them because he was too intent on getting some answers. She held her chin up and her brows bunched together. He'd seen enough distressed men in his years of fighting in the army to know she was upset about something. *Could it be the princess was having second thoughts?* Maybe she had a heart after all.

Preacher Ryan said Cole seemed a little into the whiskey, but that he recited the words clearly professing how much he cared for the maid. None of it made any sense. He blinked as the road dipped and swayed before him. He drank way too much last night and shook his head to rid the dizzy spell.

Although fetching, Matty was a maid and he'd never think to marry her or anyone else for that matter. He was resigned to living alone. There wasn't a woman within ten states who hadn't heard who his father was and thrown themselves at his feet. He wanted none of it.

It was why he'd been invited to dinner every day since he'd arrived here. He grew up with money, and even though he'd made his own way without taking a cent from his arrogant pompous father, and refused to ever do so, all they saw was the son of a Governor who came from wealth. He scowled. His cane knocked against the seat, and he set his jaw against the constant reminder of the way his life had changed. He was crippled. Injured in battle nineteen months ago, he'd been discharged from fighting and placed in the Fort to train and help organize the soldiers for the war. He had no worth.

The front line was where he belonged, commanding troops and planning attacks. He was respected there. Now he was a figure behind a desk living in an Officer's house. He refused to show any sign of defeat, and when exercising the soldiers he'd made sure to go right along with them. He paid for his excessive behaviour later when he couldn't walk a mere two feet without breaking a sweat and dry heaving from the pain.

Ice baths were the only thing that helped ease his sore limb, and since he was without a maid he'd hauled snow in from outside placing it into the metal tub himself. Alcohol lessened the pain and took away the memory of what he'd been missing out on. Matty had caught him at a time when he was at his lowest and that must've been why he'd asked her to marry him. He could think of no other reason.

He shook his head. He remembered her coming to his home, and he thought he'd struck it lucky. After the day he'd had, a roll in the hay with the little tart was just what he'd needed and no one would be the wiser. Well, he got a roll all right, and a damn wife. He gripped the reins and gave them a snap. What had he been thinking? He hadn't. He'd wanted only to bed the little witch and that was it. Now he was stuck with her and hadn't the slightest idea of how it happened. What bothered him the most was that she didn't seem to mind the arrangement of husband and wife. He was positive she'd swindled him somehow and damn it he'd find out why.

She shuddered next to him and he cursed himself for not having a wool blanket tucked under the seat. He may not want to be her husband, but he was a gentleman and propriety said to treat her with kindness.

"I will drive you to the Worthington's home where you can collect your bag."

She nodded.

"That is unless you brought one last night?" She may be a lady, but she was also a liar. He'd bet his life on it. She'd done this on purpose and he was going to get it out of her if it was the last thing he did.

"I did not bring a bag." She narrowed her brown eyes.

He gazed appreciatively at her high cheekbones, full lips and long blonde lashes. How could he not remember tasting her last night? He shifted in the seat, suddenly uncomfortable. The carriage rounded a corner and came onto Officer's Row. Whitewashed homes built to house officers and their families lined the street. The Worthington's lived at the end of the row in the largest of the pre-built homes with a barn and livestock.

He brought the carriage to a complete stop.

"You do not need to come around and help me. I can get down on my own," she said without meeting his eyes.

He flexed his jaw. "I may have a bad leg that requires me to walk with a cane, but I am not a bloody invalid." He tossed the reins onto the floor, ground his back teeth and climbed down.

Just to prove a point he didn't reach for the cane, leaving it in the carriage. She thought he wasn't capable of walking without it. He could and he did, but he'd pay for it the next day. She stood and allowed him to lift her to the ground. She smelled of baked bread, the scent clinging to her clothes and he inhaled as the distant memory from his childhood blew across his mind.

"I will wait while you go in and get your things," he said a little too close to her lips.

"Thank you, I'll be but a minute." She lifted her skirt away from the deep snow and stepped onto the walk.

He caught himself before he slipped on the ice, but couldn't stop the thrust of intense pain as it slammed into his thigh muscle. His stomach turned, and he limped toward the carriage and his cane.

"Colonel Black." The dainty voice came from behind him and he turned to see young Isabella Frank standing on the walk.

"Miss Frank." He tensed, as the pressure in his leg intensified.

"Will we be seeing you at dinner tonight?"

A thick fog of ice formed at their mouths.

He cleared his throat. "I'm sorry but—"

"Congratulations, Colonel," Mrs. Schaefer said walking up to them clad in a bright red winter frock and matching scarf.

The marriage to Matty had some value. Every home with an eligible daughter would stop calling, and that included Mrs. Schaefer.

"You went and married a maid after I offered you our Melody." Mrs. Schaefer waggled her fat finger in front of him.

"What I do with my life is none of your damn business," he said through clenched teeth. He tipped his head toward Isabella. "Tell your parents I am sorry but I have to decline our evening together." Ignoring Mrs. Schaefer, he left the two women standing in the cold and climbed into his carriage.

He blew out a long breath as the pain in his leg subsided. If he didn't have to wait for Matty, he'd be long gone by now. As it was, the two women stood on the walk in deep discussion.

Mrs. Schaefer was about as welcoming as a rabid muskrat. He'd dined at the Schaefer's home two nights ago. The woman was just short of the devil himself insisting he marry Melody. She went as far as offering him a night with the poor girl before he decided. There was a war going on. Men were heading into battle and all they could think about was pawning their daughters off to the wealthiest man dumb enough to have them. Well, now he could join the lot of them.

"Damn it."

Why did Matty marry him? It had to be the money. She was a serving girl. He was the son of Edward Black, the Governor of Michigan. He frowned. Thinking about Edward put an awful taste in his mouth. Cole hadn't seen him in five years and that wasn't long enough. Edward Black was the opposite of everything he stood for, and whenever they made acquaintance it always ended with both men yelling. He'd made his own way with no help from his father. For years he'd kept Edward's popularity and money a secret until the nosey Mrs. Schaefer had figured it out and all hell broke loose. He'd refused every woman that was thrown in his direction for a life of solidarity. He flexed his leg. The thigh burned, the muscle rubbed against the musket ball still lodged there. He'd never be the same again.

Matty couldn't get away from Colonel Black fast enough. He was so unpredictable, kind one minute and then blasting her in the next. She didn't know whether to yell back or ignore him. One thing she was sure of, he was a very bitter man. She saw that in his actions and the way he kept a safe distance from those around him. It was probably because of his ailment. When she'd decided it was him she'd wed to keep her safe, she'd never seen this abrupt side of him. He'd always been cordial and respectful whenever he dined at the Worthington's home. Yet, what she saw in him now was someone who was struggling to fit in.

She trudged through the deep snow, determination creasing her brow. The ice cracked under her feet. The old leather boots she'd worn had become stiff in the frigid wet weather, and her wool socks were soaked. She ground her teeth and buried her chin deeper into the scarf around her neck. It was ten days until Christmas. A familiar ache settled around her heart and squeezed. She missed her family, but she missed Maggie, her twin sister, more. An arctic breeze made her eyes water, and she pushed thoughts of home, and Maggie from her mind.

Mrs. Worthington owed her last month's pay. She pursed her lips. It was a far stretch that she'd even get it, since she'd left without any warning. The lady of the house despised her, and if it weren't for Abby's friendship, Mrs. Worthington would've dismissed her long ago. She was sure news had spread of her marriage to Colonel Black, and she cringed at facing her old employer.

She went around back and entered the home through the kitchen door. Last night she'd taken a bag with her to Colonel Black's, determined for her plan to work. It was still hidden under his bed, but she couldn't tell him that or he'd have known this was planned. The kitchen was empty and she made her way into the dining room. Eunice, the only other maid staffed at the Worthington's, sat at the table polishing the silver and her heart warmed. She loved the older woman, who filled the void of her mother so many miles away.

"Miss Matty, I didn't think I'd see you for days." The woman smiled showing large white teeth against dark skin.

She sat down across from her friend. Eunice had been hired just after they'd arrived at Fort Wayne and Matty adored her. Old enough to be her own mother, she'd taken Matty under her wing. She cared for the woman deeply and needed her advice.

"Eunice, I've made a mess of things."

"I heard tell you was married to handsome Colonel Black." She winked.

"Handsome is not how I'd describe him. Cranky fits his description better."

"Come now child, he is handsome as the day is long. He just needs some good lovin' to make him change his ways."

Matty groaned. Good loving was not something she was about to give. She spotted the bruises on the woman's wrists. "How have you been?"

"Oh, I'm fine, child." She swatted the air.

"Eunice, I saw the last beating. I was milking the cow when I heard you cry out."

The woman's black eyes misted and her chin quivered, before she erased all sadness from her face and replaced it with defiant rage. "Now you listen, I am fine. Ain't nothin' goin' on here that I haven't had done to me all my life."

"But it doesn't make it right." Matty reached out and caught her friends' hand in her own. "Come with me, please."

Eunice squeezed her hand. "You bess grab your bag and skedaddle, the missus is not pleased with you."

She wanted nothing more than to take the older woman from the house and the whip Mrs. Worthington used upon her frail body. "I thought maybe Mrs. Worthington would give me my last month's pay."

Eunice exhaled with a long hum. "I's don't think that's gonna happen. She is angrier than a cat tossed in the lake."

"Mother counts on that money. Werner needs it."

"I know, child. I know."

A door closed in the other room, and the clip clop of boots on the wooden floor came closer.

"You bess git, afore the missus comes in here and sees you."

Matty stood and pulled Eunice into a quick hug. "If you need anything, you know where to find me." She gave her a kiss on the cheek and was almost through the door when Mrs. Worthington walked in.

"Why, if it isn't Mrs. Black," Eleanor Worthington drawled. "Come to pay a visit did you?"

"No, Ma'am. I came to say goodbye and collect my last month's wages."

The air vanished from the room as Eleanor's face lost all pleasantries and turned dark and pointed. "You think to make a mockery of me and then ask for money?" She marched across the room and slapped Matty across the face, the sound bouncing off the walls.

The dining room spun and she concentrated on the flowered wallpaper instead of the pain in her cheek. She bowed her head and curtsied before turning to leave.

"I don't know what you're up to, but I'm determined to find out. And when I do, you'll be without a husband, a job and a reputation."

"I've done nothing wrong but marry someone who asked me."

"That is hardly how the story is being told, my dear. Colonel Black was inebriated, and he'd have to be to marry the likes of you."

Matty had nothing left to say. She gave Eunice a quick look and headed for the door. Outside, she walked toward Colonel Black's carriage.

"Where is your bag?" he asked after she'd climbed into the carriage.

She'd forgotten to grab the other one she'd left last night. There wasn't much in it, a few aprons and towels. "I…uh, Mrs. Worthington said she'd send it over."

Seated next to her, he asked, "What happened to your face?"

"Nothing. Why do you ask?" If she played dumb maybe he'd think it was nothing too and not demand answers.

He touched her cheek, the pad of his thumb rubbed across her throbbing skin. "Doesn't look like nothing."

"Well, it is." She pulled away from his touch. "Can we go now? I am freezing."

He slapped the reins and the carriage jerked forward as the horses pulled it toward her new home. Once a good distance away, she turned and stared at the home she'd been a part of for two years. She'd miss Eunice something fierce and prayed the elderly woman didn't meet the end of the leather whip again. The black woman's beatings had been kept private and away from the Fort. The General fought for the Union. He was fighting to free the slaves, while at home he and Mrs. Worthington treated Eunice as one.

She quivered thinking of the times she'd helped the other maid. Matty had taken her share of backhands from her employers, but never the whip. She couldn't help but think that the color of her skin and Abby had something to do with it.

She missed her friend, and the Worthington's only child. They'd struck up a fast friendship from the moment they met, much to Mrs. Worthington's disapproval. But Abby never did what she was told and stayed by Matty's side. Now her friend was long gone, married to a wealthy Senator twice her age.

The distance between the two homes wasn't far and when Colonel Black pulled the carriage to a stop, she didn't know what to do. To the west over the treetops she could see the Fort. The bugle and drums echoed as the soldiers practiced parade formation. She closed her eyes and let the sun warm her frosty cheeks. She thought of Eunice, the General, and the Colonel. If she hadn't found the letter she'd still be working for the Worthington's, hiding from the General and his inappropriate gestures and touches. She'd not be married to the horrible Colonel and she'd still see Eunice every day. She blinked the tears away.

"Are you okay?" he asked.

She straightened. "Yes."

He scowled. "I'm needed at the Fort."

"What time are you expected back for dinner, Colonel?"

"It's Cole and six o'clock."

She nodded and got down from the carriage without his help or offer to.

CHAPTER TWO

Cole sat outside in his carriage as white flakes lit up the black sky. For the first time in his life he was struck with a loss of words—nervous to go into his own house and see her. He stretched his leg and massaged the thigh muscle. Light cascaded from the front window and he hoped there would be dinner waiting. The last two days he'd drank his meals often to the point where he passed out, not knowing how else to deal with another denial to his appeal to fight alongside his comrades.

He couldn't understand why. Men with far worse ailments than his were still fighting; yet he, a man with a bullet in his leg was forbid it. He slammed his cane onto the floorboards. It didn't make sense. He'd proven himself worthy. Shown that he could keep up and not succumb to the injury that had struck him down almost two years ago, but it didn't matter.

There had been days he'd worked so hard he couldn't get out of bed the next morning, his leg seized and swollen, but he still persisted—still fought the plague that seemed to settle over him. He sighed and climbed down.

The smell of roasted duck and rosemary greeted him when he stepped inside. His stomach growled while he removed his hat and coat. The house had been cleaned and to his surprise decorated. Pine branches adorned the mantle over the fireplace, three red ribbons tied to it. A small Christmas tree stood in the corner of the room near the window, candles and bows sat in a pile next to it. He stared at the wooden floors reflecting his blurry image. She must've scrubbed for hours to get them so shiny. He ran a finger along the small table beside the chair he loved to read in. Not a speck of dust could be seen.

He peeked into the bedroom, the bed was made and his clothes folded. A small brown bag sat at the end of the bed unopened and he guessed it was hers. She hadn't unpacked and he wondered if that was because she was leaving? A surge of panic raced up his throat, and he coughed to rid the emotion.

"I thought we'd decorate it together," she said from behind him.

"I haven't decorated a tree since I was a child."

"Well, that is about to change."

"I don't think so. You go ahead without me."

She glanced at the floor. "Dinner is ready."

"I can smell it."

She blushed, and he tipped his head to get a better view of her face. Blonde wisps hung from her bun to frame her rosy cheeks. He dismissed thoughts of her beauty and concentrated on how she'd duped him instead.

The heat from the stove welcomed him in a warm hug as he entered the kitchen. In the year he lived at Fort Wayne, the home hadn't looked so inviting. She placed the duck on the table surrounded by mashed potatoes, gravy, and bread.

"Where did you get the food and decorations?" The cupboards were empty, there was never a need to buy anything, since most days he'd eaten at the Fort, and he didn't own a single ribbon.

"I went to the butcher and he put it on your tab." She averted her eyes from his. "The potatoes were in the pantry, and I purchased the pine from the mercantile, cut the tree from the forest out back, and used an old sheet for the ribbons."

She had been busy.

She filled a plate for him and stood off to the side.

Without looking up, he said, "Sit down, Matty."

The chair whined as she pulled it out and sat across from him.

He'd married a maid, not willingly, but married just the same. How it happened was still a blur. "I see your bag arrived."

"Yes, Eunice delivered it this afternoon."

"I was sure I'd seen it there this morning when I woke." He placed some of the duck into his mouth and almost hummed it tasted so good.

She fumbled with her fork. "It was not here."

"I see." He watched her from across the table. She sat stiff as she pushed the food around on her plate. "Would you like to tell me again how we came to be married? I cannot seem to remember anything past you entering my home last night."

She cleared her throat. "It is like I said before. I came to see if you needed anything, and we got to talking, when you begged me to marry you."

"I begged?" He laughed. Never in his thirty-eight years had he begged a woman for her company in or out of the bedroom.

"Yes. Begged." She glared at him.

"And how did I do this? Was I on my knees, Princess?"

"Do not call me that."

"Princess? It is what you've become, is it not? No more the maid, but now married to a wealthy Colonel." He chewed on his potatoes. "Now that is quite the jump, don't you think?"

"No, I do not, *Cole*."

It was the first time she'd said his name and it came with thick icicles hanging from it.

"And why is that?"

"I owe you nothing." She stood, plate in hand.

"You owe me a damn explanation," he growled.

Her brown eyes watered, and he didn't miss the quiver in her pert chin. She turned from him and placed the plate onto the counter.

"You wanted me," she whispered and he had to lean in to hear.

"Yes I did, in my bed, not as my wife."

She spun and fire shot from her eyes. "I will not stand here and be ridiculed by you any longer. You asked me. You begged me. There is nothing more to say."

He leaned over the table. "There is plenty to say."

"The past is but a pebble in my own shoe." She balanced the leftover duck and potatoes in her arms.

"The past you speak of happened yesterday. So tell of it or you'll be sorry." He needed to know what happened. Why the hell he couldn't remember. Then it struck him. He'd been drugged; the headache, the dizziness it was all explained now.

"There are far worse things out there that frighten me than you," she said.

"You drugged me." He pointed.

Her face lost all color and he knew he'd struck the truth.

"You put something in my drink."

"Nonsense! Why would I do such a thing?" Her back was to him and he went to stand behind her, his dinner forgotten.

"For money, as I've said."

She spun slamming into his chest.

He caught her arms and squeezed.

"I...I did not drug you."

"I've drank plenty more than I did last night without the side effects I experienced upon waking today. You put something in my glass." He gave her a shake. "Now what was it?"

Matty didn't know how to answer. He'd guessed what she'd done and it hadn't taken him long. "What kind of person do you think I am?"

"One who would drug a wealthy man and trick him into marriage!"

His dark eyes bore into hers and she had to look away before she confessed. "Contrary to what you think, I did not drug you." *I am going to burn.*

She pulled from his grasp and when he advanced she shrunk into herself, fear knocking the air from her lungs.

He stopped and stepped away from her. His arms fell to his sides. "I am not going to hurt you."

"It is what the wealthy do, is it not?"

"The Worthington's treated you so?"

"You are not aware of how a maid is treated, a wealthy man such as yourself?" She folded her arms for protection from his fists.

"General Worthington never seemed the type."

"O' what a goodly outside falsehood hath."

"Shakespeare?" He wasn't adept in the art of poetry but he knew she was and used them often.

She nodded.

"I do not hit women, maids or otherwise."

She believed him, not because she had to but because she needed to. He was her only hope. She placed her hand in her apron pocket and felt the letter she'd found on the step upon returning from the butchers, threatening her life if she didn't turn over the paper she'd found. She wanted to tell him the truth, but was scared he'd throw her out onto the street with no protection. She couldn't chance it.

"I'd never hurt you Matty, no matter what you've done to me."

A thick brown curl streaked with grey fell onto his forehead and he brushed it aside. His broad shoulders relaxed and his jagged features softened. She'd not seen this side of him and had to withdraw before she fell into his charm and confessed all her sins.

"I've done nothing but try to be what a wife should."

"Ah, Matty. I think you know what I am talking about. We are not suited. I wish to marry no one. An annulment would solve both our problems."

An annulment? She'd told him they'd consummated and he still suggested it? "What if I'm with child?" The words were out before she could stop them. There was no time for remorse. *I need him.*

Concern drew his thick brows together. He placed his head in his hands rubbing his eyes before he looked at her again. "When is your monthly?"

"One week." This was true. She'd tried to lie and tell him three weeks but the words got stuck in her throat. Now she prayed a week could give her enough time to find another way out of this mess.

"That's Christmas."

She nodded.

"If by then you're not with child will you agree to annul this marriage?"

"Yes," she whispered.

He bowed, gave her one last look and walked past her into the sitting room where he lit a cigar. The smoke ascended above his head in a thick haze.

She'd just walked herself into another lie and this time there was no getting out of it. One week was all she had to either convince Cole to stay married, or face the consequences that waited for her without his protection. If she hadn't found the letter, hadn't read the incriminating words scribbled upon it, she'd not be lying to save her life while ruining another's. She couldn't blame Cole for his hatred, or his questions. He'd been tricked—drugged with no memory as to what took place hours before. Now he was stuck with a wife he did not want, and a baby that will never exist.

Half of her wanted to fall at his feet and beg him to help her; while the other wanted to maintain the façade she'd so carefully planned. By Christmas they'd part ways, he living the life of a wealthy bachelor and she on the run or worse, dead. She didn't know whom to trust and only knew of a few people listed on the damaging letter but there were plenty more.

While in town today she swore someone was following her, so instead of lingering to browse the shops, she headed home and found the letter nailed to the door written in blood. They were going to kill her if she didn't hand it over. Now more than ever she was certain she'd done the right thing in drugging Cole into marriage. If she returned the letter like they asked, her life would be no more. What she needed to do was find a way to get the letter to Cole's father before it was too late.

She sat at the kitchen table with her book, *The Courtship of Miles Standish*, by Henry Wadsworth Longfellow. The book lay open but she couldn't seem to concentrate on the words within it. All she could think about were the sleeping arrangements tonight. There was no other room within the small home and she'd have to sleep in the same bed as Cole. She took a sip of her tea and placed her chin in her palm. He'd rejected her in every way possible. She couldn't blame him. He didn't want this any more than she did.

How could she possibly think he'd agree to the arrangement she'd forced upon him? She'd only thought of herself when she'd hatched the devious crime. Guilt swirled around her stomach and squeezed. If Pa were alive he'd have lectured her until the cows came home. She thought of Ma and Werner and how they'd be looking for the money she and Maggie sent every month. There'd be none from her and she prayed Ma had some stashed away for Werner's medication.

She hadn't been home in almost two years. Had Werner grown into the young man she imagined him to be? She pictured him to look like Pa, tall and lean with piercing blue eyes. She hoped Ma was able to rest now knowing her daughters were helping as much as they could.

She'd written letters to both Ma and Maggie, but hadn't received a reply from either. With the war in full swing she didn't even know if they'd gotten them. How she'd love to hear from Maggie. Her sister had a way of brightening her day and a letter would do the trick.

"It's time to turn in," Cole stood in the doorway to the kitchen.

She closed her book and held it tight so he wouldn't see her hands shaking.

"There is only one room, so we'll have to share the bed." He paused. "I've got a nice fire going and the room is warm."

She gave him a small smile and followed him into the bedroom. She faced the wall while he stripped down into his underwear and crawled beneath the thick quilt. She wasn't about to take her clothes off in front of him. She wrung her hands together.

"Could you please close your eyes while I undress?" She went to her bag and dug out her nightgown.

"No."

She froze and chewed on her bottom lip.

"According to you, we slept together last night. I've already seen you naked, Princess." He winked.

The bastard wasn't going to make this easy for her. Her cheeks heated, and she turned her back to him to undress. She left her pantaloons and camisole on slipping the nightgown over her head. Leaving her hair in its braid, she pulled back the quilt and lay down beside him stiff as a board.

He rolled toward her and propped his arm up resting his head in his hand. "Why are you so nervous?"

"I am not nervous," she whispered.

"For someone who declares that I was inside you last night you're sure fidgety."

She stared at the ceiling. "It was dark."

"It still happened." He traced his finger down the side of her face.

"I'm exhausted. Good night." She rolled over facing the wall placing her back to him.

"Yes, conniving and lying can take its toll on a person. Good night." He blew the candle out and the room was black.

She couldn't help the long sigh as it blew past her lips and she buried her head into the pillow. Within a few minutes Cole snored beside her and she relaxed her whole body releasing the tension from her neck. Uncomfortable with her pantaloons and camisole on underneath her nightgown, she inched out of the bed and removed them so that she just wore the white flannel gown. Cole lay on his back breathing heavy, and she crawled back in beside him. She wondered what had happened to his leg. Had he been injured during battle? She'd seen him walk without his cane, and even though he favoured the left leg he could still keep his balance. This morning when he'd come around to get her, she noticed his gait was more prominent than when they had first gotten into the carriage. Was it because of the cold? Did the weather affect the function of his leg?

She lit the lamp beside the bed and turned the wick down low, so it cast the room in an orange glow. Curiosity shoved her to raise the quilt, pulling it back so she could see his leg. A long scar drew a nasty pattern from the middle of his thigh up to his hip.

"All you had to do was ask, Princess."

She gasped, dropped the quilt, rolled over and blew out the lantern.

He chuckled.

Thank goodness the room was black, she was sure she'd turned a hundred shades of red. She buried her head in the pillow and willed herself to sleep.

CHAPTER THREE

Matty stood away from the door, arms folded tightly across her chest. Three loud knocks shook the wooden frame. Whoever stood on the other side wanted in and she had no intention of opening the door. *What if it was them?* She squeezed the muscles in her arms tighter. *Knock, knock.* She glanced behind her. The banging was sure to wake Cole. A loud knock followed by a kick to the bottom of the door vibrated the inside walls and she took a step back. Her throat thick with fear, she reached out a shaky hand as she moved backward along the wall.

"What in hell are you doing?" Cole came from the bedroom, his shirt unbuttoned and his pants open at the waist. Dark brows furrowed into a frightening glare.

She stepped aside when another knock shook the door.

He yanked it open. "What is it?"

"A letter, Sir."

Matty watched from the corner as Cole took the paper and opened it. He groaned as he released a long breath. "Tell him to go to hell."

"He...he said it is urgent, Sir."

"I don't give a damn."

"He said to tell you he wishes to discuss your position on the battle field."

Matty watched as Cole stiffened while pondering the soldier's last words.

"We will be there this afternoon," he muttered.

The young soldier nodded and left

"Get dressed, Princess. We've been summoned."

"By whom?"

"Edward Black."

Matty let her shoulders fall while releasing a sigh. She'd been trying to figure out a way to get the letter to Governor Black and now she no longer had to worry. He wanted to see them. She was sure that once he saw the letter, he'd help her. Soon she'd annul her marriage to Cole and have her life back.

Matty sat rigid on the seat trying to keep her balance as the carriage rolled over the uneven road. Cole hadn't uttered a single word since telling her his father wished to see them and she was enjoying the silence. For now, he wasn't hounding her about the other night. The past two days had been trying and she'd begun to second-guess the scheme she'd plotted. Cole despised her, making it perfectly clear how he felt. Last night while lying in bed, she'd contemplated packing her small bag and leaving. She'd made a huge mistake in thinking he'd be able to offer her protection. *How could he, when he doesn't even know what I need protection from?*

She peeked at him. Even with his gait he posed a strong threat, one that didn't back down from anyone or anything. No one seemed to push Cole too far, the General included, and she was sure he'd be strong enough mentally and physically to help her out of this mess, even if he didn't know what it was. She needed his stature and his father's position offered the protection she required. People would think twice before going up against the grumpy Colonel, and no one would challenge the Governor.

She'd watched Cole on his many visits to the Worthington's place. He and the General often spoke of war politics, and she'd witnessed the decent side of him while eavesdropping. She couldn't trust a mere stranger with her life. She needed to find someone with the same beliefs as her. If the letter fell into the wrong hands, innocent lives would be taken.

When she'd found out Cole's father was the Governor of Michigan she'd become even more intrigued. Why wasn't he running for office or working as a lawyer like his father? Instead he'd enlisted in the army wanting to serve his country. It was quite clear that Cole didn't have fond thoughts for his father, and she wondered if the feeling was mutual. Did Governor Black approve of his son's decision to take a different path than his own? How could Cole hate his own kin?

When she thought of Pa, emptiness filled her soul. He'd been gone three years, and yet it only seemed like yesterday when they'd lowered him into the ground. Walter Becker was a feisty German with strong beliefs and a good moral ethic, which he instilled in his children. He prophesied the coming war years before it happened. A School Master, he also attended anti-slavery meetings which led to his demise. She wiped a cold tear from her cheek. More now than ever she needed her father's advice.

She shivered. The fort was a good hour's ride from the city and she was glad Cole thought to bring a blanket. She tucked the end under her right leg. Light flakes wet her cheeks and clung to her lashes. She folded her mitted hands on her lap and peeked at him beside her. His face held a grim expression and every so often he worked his jaw.

"Do you see your father often?"

"No." He slapped the reins.

"Why is that?"

His face turned sour. "We do not see eye to eye."

She didn't push him further.

The snow-covered field on her right hosted a view of the Fort's outside walls and the roof of the barracks. She watched as a deer bolted from the forest, trampling hoof prints all over the snowy landscape. The frosted elms in front of them made way for a glorious sight. She sighed, feeling at ease for the first time in weeks. The carriage drew closer to the small thick of woods when two men on horseback wearing burlap sacks over their heads emerged from the forest.

Oh, no! Stomach in knots, she moved closer to Cole, every muscle in her body flexed. *They found me.* She searched their surroundings for somewhere they might escape, but with open field on their right, the river to their left, and forest in front of them, they were doomed.

The riders approached, pistols drawn.

"I don't suppose you have anything to do with our visitors?" Cole ground out.

She didn't answer. He'd guessed the truth and there was no point in defending herself. She looked again at the area around them. Forward into the forest was their only chance.

"We want the girl," the man on the left yelled.

"Why is that?" Cole asked.

What was he doing? Now wasn't the time for questions. They needed to think of an escape route.

"She has something that belongs to us," the man on the right replied.

There was something about his voice—the pitchy up and down baritone. She'd never heard anything like it and wondered if Cole had noticed. She stared hard at the small holes cut into the sacks for their eyes trying to see any resemblance to the many men she'd seen while living at the Fort.

"What would that be?" Cole asked.

"That is none of your damn business, Colonel," he said.

"You know who I am," Cole said with a smile.

The conversation between Cole and her abductor's was irritating, and she pinched his arm to get him to stop. When he didn't look at her she pinched him harder.

"Do you mind, Princess? I am trying to figure this out," he muttered so they wouldn't hear.

"Really, because it looks to me like you're about ready to have tea and scones," she hissed.

"Everyone knows who you are," the man on the left said.

Cole nodded.

"Just give us the girl and no one gets hurt."

"If I hand her over, what will you do with her?" Cole asked.

Matty inhaled deep, the frigid air burning her nostrils. Contrary to what Cole told her, soon she'd be whisked away by the masked men. She couldn't allow that to happen. Without another rational thought, she stood from her seat and shouted, "Oh, the agony of my soul found vent in one loud, long and final scream of despair."

The men stopped talking to stare at her.

"Not now, Princess."

"What is it she is saying?" one of the men asked.

She pointed to the hooded man on the right. "That man is not truly brave who is afraid either to seem or to be, when it suits him, a coward."

"My wife is, well, how do you say, a little crazy."

"Haven't I told you that what you mistake for madness is but over-acuteness of the senses?" she spat. They wouldn't take her without a fight.

"You don't want her. She's somewhat of a bother if you know what I mean."

"We have orders. Dead or alive."

"I see," Cole said. "Well, then we have a problem."

"We have no trouble with you, Sir. We want the girl. That is all."

"I cannot hand her over. As much as I'd love to. I spoke vows, even if I cannot remember them or my bloody wedding night, she is my wife and I protect what is mine."

"I'm sorry too, Sir," the man on the right said as he raised his pistol and aimed it at Cole.

"You're going to shoot me, Soldier?"

Soldier? How did Cole know? Matty stared at the two men again. They didn't look like soldiers, but she guessed most every man here was one. A shot went off and the acrid smell of gunpowder filled her nostrils. The man on the left fell from his horse, and Matty turned to see smoke coming from Cole's drawn pistol. The other soldier shot back but missed, hitting the wooden seat between them.

Cole snapped the reins several times off the horses' backs and turned the team left to put space between them and the other rider. "Hold on."

She grabbed onto the side of the seat as the carriage leaned to the side. The masked man fired at them as they turned.

"Take the reins," Cole yelled, not waiting for her reply as he threw the leather straps at her.

She fumbled with the reins as the carriage jerked left and she fell forward onto her knees. Pain erupted in her legs upon impact with the floorboards and she reached for the leather straps gripping them tight within her palm. Another shot rang out and she hunkered down too scared to sit back up on the seat. She needed to steer them out of this mess. She took a deep breath, prayed for courage, and sat upright on the seat. *I can do this.*

"Yaw, yaw," she yelled.

She glanced at Cole, smoke billowing from his pistol as he fired at the man chasing them. She jerked forward followed by a piercing pain in her right shoulder. Her arm ached, the flesh screamed and her fingers went numb. She swayed toward Cole. The scenery spun before her and she reached out to steady herself. The throbbing in her shoulder grew more intense and she closed her eyes to stop the bile crawling up her throat. She released the reins and reached for her arm. Warmth filled her mitten, and she glanced down to see that it was covered in blood.

Cole shoved her to the carriage floor. "Stay down!"

She couldn't. She needed to get out of the carriage. She had to find help. She stood, jerked left and then right, knocking into Cole.

"I said stay down, damn it." He shoved her aside with a glare.

Her stomach lurched. The bumpy ride, the twists, the pain in her arm all spun around her and she placed her head against him.

"I don't feel so well," she said. The horse's backs blurred and she slumped to the side passed out.

Cole caught Matty just as she fell forward and banged her forehead on the rail. With one hand on the reins, he laid her across his feet on the floor of the carriage. The rider had run out of bullets and turned away.

Cole steered them into the forest and took a hard left stopping to wait and see if the man followed. Minutes stretched into a half hour as he waited pistol loaded and aimed at the entrance into the woods.

He wanted nothing more than to give chase, but he couldn't leave Matty. He glanced down at her and saw the blood seeping from her coat. Terror seized him and he placed his fingers to her neck to check for a pulse. He let out a loud sigh when he felt her heart beat. Without a care for the frigid temperature, he stripped the coat from her to have a look. The bullet ripped the flesh from the side of her shoulder, but didn't go through. She was lucky, but he needed to get her home and clean the wound before it festered and infection set in. They were still a good distance from Detroit, and he couldn't chance it if the man came back with more riders. He placed the coat back over her and covered her with the blanket.

His leg thrummed to the beat of his heart, and he stretched it out to ease the ache there. It was no use. The temperature was well below zero and his heroism had cost him plenty. The damn limb was proving to be more and more of a bother. He'd done what any man would do when being shot at by masked men and now he'd pay for it. He'd ignored the warning signs his thigh gave him, hell bent on protecting them instead.

He turned the carriage toward home. Who were the men, and what did Matty have that they wanted? He pulled the team to a stop where blood smeared the snow. A fallen rider had lay here, but he was gone now.

"Damn it."

He hoped to at least put a face to one of the men. He found it interesting that they never denied it when he'd called them soldiers. He slapped the reins urging the horses to move at a steady speed. He glanced down at Matty. What was she hiding? This had to be the reason she'd tricked him into marriage. But why him? Why not some other man? Questions filled his head and he had no answers for them. He flexed his jaw. He would soon. He'd damn well make sure of it.

Matty opened her eyes and stared at a white ceiling. She could hear someone moving around in the other room, and without guessing she'd known it was Cole. His poor leg slid across the hardwood floors as he walked with his cane. She shifted on the bed and nearly came undone when a sharp pain raced down her arm to throb in her fingers. She'd been shot. The two men chasing them earlier had wanted to kill her. She took a slow breath trying to ease the heaviness in her chest, but it didn't work. Her heart galloped as sweat gathered at her temples. She could've died. Cole could've died. The room grew cold and she knew before glancing at the door he was standing there.

"Glad to see you're awake, Princess," he growled.

If she hadn't already been panicking from the day's event she was sure to be now. *What will I tell him? He's bound to ask questions.* She closed her eyes.

"I know you're awake." He moved beside her. "Stop with the games and tell me what the hell is going on."

She squeezed her eyes shut and mustered up the courage to face him. "There are some secrets that do not permit themselves to be told," she whispered.

He raised a brow.

She held her lips closed refusing to say more.

"That's it? You're going to spout more of your Shakespeare? You're not going to tell me why you've tricked me into marriage and why the hell someone wants you dead!"

She pulled her eyes from his and focused on the armoire in the room. She couldn't tell him the truth. He'd go mad. What if he tossed her out on her rear, or worse, what if he didn't believe her? She needed to see Governor Black. He was the only one she could trust.

"Aren't you afraid?" Cole asked leaning across her so she couldn't look away.

She blinked back the tears that threatened to fall and stared right through him.

"Talk to me!"

"What is it you wish me to say?"

"What were those men looking for?"

She looked away.

"They said you have something they need. What is it?"

"I cannot tell you."

"Then tell me who those men were."

"I do not know."

"The hell you don't." He pushed on the bed and stood.

She didn't miss the pull in his face when he shifted onto his bad leg. *Tell him.* She couldn't.

"If I knew who those men were I'd tell you." That much was true.

He snarled low in his throat. "Tell me your secrets."

"I have none." *Liar.*

"The quote you spouted says otherwise."

"Let no such man be trusted."

"Trust? That's what this is about? You don't trust me?"

"I do not know you."

His face turned red and he ran his hand through his hair. "You trusted me well enough to spread your legs."

She gasped.

"You tricked me into marriage and yet you cannot trust me?"

"Contrary to what you think, there was no trickery."

"Bull shit."

"Think what you want. I married you because you asked."

"That's it then? You defeat death today only because I was there to save you, yet you haven't the decency to tell me why?"

She tipped her chin. She'd said enough already. How could she have ever thought Cole Black would be easy to manipulate. He'd seen right through her to the liar that she was.

"I am not only stuck with a wife I do not want, but a relation to Delilah herself."

She opened her mouth.

He turned and limped from the room.

Once he was gone, she let the tears fall from her lashes to soak her face. She'd ruined Cole's life and almost gotten him killed in the process. If Pa were alive he'd shake his head at his daughter's behavior. *You weren't raised to tell lies, Kitten. Lies are the root of all evil. No good can come from them.* The many sermons Walter Becker preached to his family filled her head. *Do unto others as you would have them do unto you.*

"I'm sorry, Pa. I know I've let you down."

But there was no other way. She couldn't tell Cole. Lives depended on her to keep this secret, only telling the one person who could make a difference.

"What am I going to do?"

She wished Maggie were here. The smarter one of the two sisters, she would know what to do. Her throat grew thick and she raised her good arm to wipe away the tears. It was a week before Christmas. She had no money, a mockery of a marriage, and was living on borrowed time. Her shoulder burned when she rolled onto her good side. She needed to see Edward Black, and soon.

Cole closed the door after James left. The colored soldier was his right hand man. He trusted him like no other. James had returned a half hour ago with a reply from Edward. The Governor hadn't summoned him, but he'd like to extend his congratulations on the wedding and will send a gift soon. Cole crumpled up the paper that bore Edward's seal and sat down in his favorite chair. He hadn't thought to check the seal on the note this morning. He'd been so angry that Matty hadn't answered the door, he'd all but flung the note back at the soldier.

If Edward hadn't called on them, then they'd been set up. He lifted the lid on the cigar box and took one, propping it between his lips. He tasted the tobacco on his tongue and rolled the cigar back and forth across his mouth.

Someone had to know about his requests to fight in the field alongside his men to have suggested that Edward wished to discuss it. They would've known about the turmoil between father and son as well to have such a response. He flexed his jaw. The men today were intent on taking Matty or killing her. He frowned. She was a maid. What could she possibly know or have that would find her running from men who wanted her dead? Did it have something to do with General Worthington? Is that why she ran from the house into a stranger's arms? He couldn't see it; the General was harmless. He straightened remembering when Matty came back from the Worthington home with a red welt on her cheek. Maybe he was wrong. He'd question the General about how they disciplined their staff.

He glanced in the direction of the bedroom. She had the answers, but he didn't know how to get them from her if she didn't trust him. She was scared. He'd seen it in her eyes and the quiver of her chin. Yet, she'd married him—a complete stranger. How did she know he wasn't one of the men hunting her? He lit the cigar and inhaled the heady smoke letting it fill his lungs, before blowing it out in a thick cloud.

His mind replayed the many dinners he'd had with General

Worthington and his family. He'd been over for roasted venison when he finally noticed Matty, taken aback at the clear brown eyes, pale skin, and blonde hair. Most maids bore black circles under their eyes and had skeletal frames. This was not the case with Matty. She stood regally to the side and he thought she belonged in a castle the way she held herself. He'd never heard her speak until the morning he'd found her in his bed.

What is it she wanted? It had to be something important for her to trick a stranger into marriage. If it was protection of some sort she needed, why him? He was a cripple damn it and he had other pressing matters, like finding his way into battle. He didn't need to be tied to a girl in danger.

He scowled. He'd been tricked twice in one week; once by Matty, and this morning by not checking the letter for Edward's seal. *There are some secrets that do not permit themselves to be told.* What did she mean? Maybe she was bound by some law and couldn't tell him. He shook his head at his own foolishness. She almost died and yet she still refused to utter one word of why the men wanted to kill her. Cole ground his teeth together.

"I need to use the privy," she said from behind him.

"Then use it."

"I...I cannot without your help."

He smashed the end of the cigar into the glass bowl, heaved a loud sigh, turned toward her and stopped dead in his tracks. Her blonde hair hung past her waist in loose curls. He'd ripped off the arm of her dress to clean the wound. But as she stood before him now, the fabric hung, torn from the seams offering a glimpse of her chemise and the rosy nipple beneath it. He held his breath.

"I cannot go with the use of only one arm."

Her soft voice pulled his eyes from her breasts to the injured arm bound to her stomach with an old sheet. He could see how she'd need his help.

"I see." He coughed while reaching for his cane. He could go without it, but needed a distraction from Matty and her exposed skin.

"I will need you to undo the knot at my neck." She turned her back toward him.

He swept her hair to the side, refusing the urge to place his face within the thick waves and inhale. The knot wasn't tight and he had it undone within seconds.

"When you are finished I will clean the wound again."

She nodded.

CHAPTER FOUR

Cole watched as hundreds of soldiers practiced line formation and bugle drills on the grass in front of the barracks. Soon the men would be departing to fight in the war with only a quarter of them returning. The others would spend months in the hospital healing from bullet wounds and amputations.

He gripped the handle of his cane. His job was to train soldiers and bring them into the battlefield as armed men ready to kill. He'd fought in many wars over the years against the Comanche, Crow, and Apache. He'd taken his skills for granted—thought he knew the Indians' way of attack until the Pah Ute War in 1860. He'd been ambushed, and if he hadn't known any better he'd of sworn his platoon was set up. Three Native bands, Paiutes, Shoshone, and Bannock had declared war on the United States and his men were the first to be sent in.

He'd remember that day for the rest of his life; a hundred and five men under his command, and when the smoke cleared there were twenty-five left. Injured by three muskets, he prayed to die but hadn't been as lucky. He flexed his leg. If he moved it a bit to the right he could feel the bullet rub against the bone.

"Good afternoon, Colonel," General Worthington said as he entered Cole's office.

"General."

"I heard tell you up and married my maid last week." The man smiled and his fat cheeks squished his mouth making his white moustache protrude past his lips, to cover his teeth.

"Yes, I suppose that is true." Cole watched as the rotund General stood beside him staring out the window.

"It's too bad. Matty was a good girl and quite good at her duties."

He remembered the mark on Matty's face the day he'd taken her to the Worthington's and anger burned in his chest. "How long was she employed with you?"

"A little over two years."

"You brought her to the Fort then?" He hadn't known, and assumed Matty had lived here being employed with the Worthington's only a short time.

"Yes, she worked for us in Fort Leavenworth. Needed the job to help pay for her sick brother's medication."

He glanced up. "Sick brother?"

"I see you know nothing about your new wife. Might the rumors be true then? A drunken Colonel and a desperate maid?" The General laughed while holding his round belly.

He opened and closed his fist over the knob of his cane. The General wasn't known to hold back what he thought. The truth of how he saw things spilled from his lips on a regular basis. He couldn't figure if it was a blessing or a curse.

"I don't give a damn what the rumors are, and just so you know, Sir," he took a step toward the General, "I know enough about Matty to be aware of how you and your wife treated her."

"We treated Mathilda like we've treated all our maids, to know what is expected of them, and when they do not follow through, what the consequences are."

"I presume, you are speaking of your fists, *Sir*."

"Don't act so surprised, old boy. It is what the wealthy do."

He didn't remember much of his youth or how his father treated the staff, but he did remember Greta, his nanny. She was a sweet German lady who loved him as if he were her own.

"The wealthy need a lesson in propriety." He turned from the General.

"Nonsense. It has always been and will always be this way. No use in trying to change things now."

"They are women!" He could feel his face heat and his chest grow tight. General Worthington had always been hard headed, but he never expected this from him. Then again he'd never had personal dealings with the man. When having dinner at his home their conversations consisted of politics and war, nothing personal was ever discussed. Cole couldn't shake the feeling that all this time he'd been baited to think the Worthington's were respectable people.

"They are maids—lowlifes that will never sit at the same table as the rest of us." The General eyed Cole. "That is unless we marry them." He burst out laughing.

"That's enough."

"Why on earth would you marry her? Surely she would've spread her legs for you and if not, that's what being of higher esteem is for." His round belly shook as he let out a boisterous laugh.

Had the General forced himself on Matty? His stomach turned and before he could catch himself he slammed his fist onto the desk. He'd have much rather planted his knuckles in the Generals fat face, but he'd be stripped of all colors and cast out of the army for good.

"We are done here, Sir," he couldn't keep the anger from his voice.

"I should charge you for her," General Worthington went on. His eyes shot daggers at Cole. "She was mine first."

"She is not a slave." All reason and rank left him and he smashed his cane across the windowsill, snapping the end off. "Have you forgotten what we are fighting for?"

"Yes, yes." He turned toward the door and lowered his voice. "Calm yourself, Colonel. It isn't wise to lose your head over such circumstances. We both know what this war is about and why we are here."

Cole leaned against the wall, his leg hurt like hell. He folded his arms, every muscle in his body tense. He'd thought of telling the General about the attack on Matty the other day, to get some advice, but instead turned the conversation to the war.

"Have any soldiers departed for Fredericksburg?"

"A regiment left yesterday morning."

Shit, he'd never be able to find the soldiers who shot Matty if they were a part of the regiment. Another thought struck him. "Why wasn't I asked to command them?"

"Until I receive the papers from the President stating you've been released into active duty, you remain here."

He ran his back teeth together and exhaled through his nose.

A rap at the door halted the conversation and General Worthington hurried to open it.

Major Smith stood in the hall and saluted them. "General, you are needed in artillery."

"Thank you, Major."

The man nodded saluted again and left.

Cole was relieved the conversation between them was over. Another minute with his superior and things were bound to turn nasty.

"If you ever tire of the girl, I'll gladly take her back." His eyes belied what he'd do to Matty, and Cole advanced not caring about rank, and the consequences.

The General stepped back and sent him a scathing glare. "Watch yourself, boy. If it wasn't for your father, you'd be locked away in a military prison."

The threat poured over Cole soaking him in a reality he knew the General could enforce. If he thought he'd get away with it, he'd beat the pompous ass to a bloody pulp for allowing the words to pass his thick lips.

"I don't take to threats, General," he snarled. "But if you speak of my wife in such a way again I'll do more than lay my hands on you."

After the door closed, Cole grabbed the broken cane and smashed it over his desk sending pieces of wood all over the office.

"Shit."

Matty had told him the cane was splintered, and he'd lost his temper breaking the stick into bits. The hidden dagger lay on the floor beside the pieces of wood. It was the only thing left intact. He picked up the thin knife, and put it in the drawer of his desk. Two letters signed by the President stared back at him and he made a fist. Both denials to fight alongside his men. He lifted a letter and stared at the Presidential seal. Why wouldn't the President approve his request? He crumbled the letter and squeezed it within his hand.

A strong desire to see Matty came over him and he grabbed his coat and scarf from the hook.

Matty sat in Cole's chair sewing a skirt for Mrs. Kindle three doors down. The Major and his wife were expecting and she was desperate for a few new skirts. She needed the money and when Mrs. Kindle approached her this morning with the fabric from the store tucked under her arm, she couldn't have been happier.

Mrs. Kindle wasn't like any of the other women she'd come across while being employed with the Worthington's. She didn't even own a maid. Close to Matty's age, the woman was a petite brunette with dark blue eyes and a warm smile. The money she'd make from the two skirts and blouse would be enough to send home to Ma for Werner. She bit the inside of her lip to stop her chin from trembling. She missed them so. *Mag, I long for your advice.* She wiped away a tear.

A soft knock at the door startled her, and she pulled back the curtain on the front window to see who it was. Relief softened her shoulders when she recognized Corporal Davis, and opened the door.

"Mrs. Black, a soldier left this letter for the Colonel," he said.

"Thank you, Corporal. Won't you please come in and have a warm cup of coffee?"

The snow was falling and she pulled the shawl tight around her. The poor man stood outside most of the day. Cole had decided that after the shooting two days before she needed someone to stand guard until he could think of another solution. He introduced her to Corporal James Davis, a colored soldier who he trusted. Corporal Davis was soft spoken with kind eyes and Matty liked him immediately. Yesterday the wind was so strong she was sure he'd turn into a snowman if she hadn't coaxed him inside to warm by the fire.

"Please, come in Corporal."

"I better stay at my post, but thank you just the same, ma'am."

"You are not going back out there without a warm cup of coffee to take with you."

He smiled showing straight white teeth. "That's mighty kind of you, ma'am."

Matty put the telegram on the mantle and went into the kitchen to fetch him a coffee. She inhaled the faint smell of cigar and thought of Cole.

He'd kept his distance only coming near to sleep in the bed beside her. Guilt consumed her and she fought with herself over telling him the truth. He'd suffered from the shootout too and for that she was greatly sorry. His gait was more prominent the last two days, and when she asked if he needed anything she was met with an angry growl.

She didn't know what else to do other than to tell him the truth and pray he'd understand. As it was, she didn't think she'd meet Governor Black any time soon, and time was of the essence. At least the letter was safe. She'd hidden it where no one would find it.

"Here you are." She smiled brightly.

"Ah, Ma'am you are too kind to a colored boy like myself."

"Colored? Are you purple, Corporal Davis?"

He chuckled and then his face turned serious. "No I ain't, Ma'am. But my skin is darker than yours and there the line is drawn."

"I say there is no darkness but ignorance. You are made of flesh and blood are you not?"

He nodded.

"Your heart beats with love, hate, forgiveness, sadness?"

"Yes, Ma'am."

"Then I ask you, what is so different from you or I but the color of our skin?"

Corporal Davis stood half way in the door, cold air fogged around him, as he stared at the floor.

Matty reached out and placed her hand on his shoulder. Dark eyes met hers and she swallowed back the sorrow she saw there.

"You are a special one, Miss Matty. The Colonel is lucky for it."

She squeezed his arm. "My father taught me that all men are equal, Corporal. The color of your skin does not dictate the man inside."

"Your father, he was a smart man."

"Yes, he was and he died fighting for what he believed in."

"I'm sorry, Ma'am."

"Don't be, I know he is always with me."

He held up his cup. "I best get back to duty. You have a nice evening and thank you for the coffee."

"You too, Corporal and thank you for being here." She closed the door softly behind him and went back to her sewing.

The front door swung open followed by a cold breeze and Matty glanced up from her sewing to see Cole enter the house.

"I wasn't expecting you for another hour."

He grunted and limped toward the closet. Opening it, he pulled out another cane.

"Where is your old one?" she asked and placed the fabric to the side.

"I broke it."

"I am not surprised with all the banging you do with it."

He scowled.

She glanced away unable to look into his eyes and see everything she'd done to him. He poured himself a drink and sat down across from her. His cheeks were red from the cold, and his mouth turned down into a nasty frown.

"Your leg is bothering you."

He took a long sip before answering her. "When it is cold the muscle seizes and I cannot rid the pain."

"You have overworked it as well."

He didn't answer.

"I will heat some water and you can soak in a hot bath after supper. It will help ease the muscle."

"Why didn't you tell me General Worthington laid his hands on you?"

Taken aback at his abrupt question, she fiddled with the needle and thread before answering him. "It was no concern of yours."

"I came to realize today that I know nothing about you, other than the simple fact that you're very adept in the art of deception."

"You've never asked and I did not deceive you," she hissed.

"So you've said. However, there are certain things that cannot be explained."

She stood. "I need to see to dinner."

"Sit." His voice left no room for challenge and she lowered slowly into her seat.

"What is it you want from me?" she asked, tired of playing this game with him. Why couldn't he just accept they were married and be done with it? Instead, he had to berate her every chance he got.

"I want the truth."

"I have told you the truth."

"No, you haven't. I've had to guess most of it and even then you still will not tell me." He took another drink. "What is it that you're running from and what does it have to do with General Worthington?"

Had he found the letter? She'd hidden it so well. She dropped the fabric and when she picked it up, the needle dug into her finger. She placed her bleeding thumb into her mouth before she met his gaze.

"I need an answer, Matty."

"I...I—"

The sound of glass shattering and a gust of frigid air filled the room.

Cole dived from his chair knocking her to the floor with him.

"Stay down," he yelled.

She was shaking so badly she couldn't move even if she wanted to. Blinding pain shot through her shoulder and she glanced at her injured arm to see blood soak her dress. Snow blew in from the broken window and she sought out Cole immediately.

He was crouched by the windowsill, pistol drawn as bluffs of cold air puffed from his mouth. Tiny pieces of glass lay everywhere and she tried to ease the pain in her shoulder by rolling onto her other side, when a shard of glass poked her leg.

"James. Where is James," she called, ashamed she hadn't thought of the soldier before now.

"I sent him home when I arrived." He stood and put his pistol in the holster hanging from his hips. He went to her and held out his hand. "They must've thought you were alone."

She took his hand and he pulled her up. She couldn't contain the groan as it passed her lips from the intense pain in her shoulder.

"Are you okay? Are you hurt?" He held her away from him as he scanned her body. "Your shoulder, it's bleeding."

"Yes, I know. I am fine." She smoothed her skirt and stepped away from him. "What came through the window?"

"My guess is a rock." He searched the floor of broken glass, wood chips, and snow kicking the debris as he went. The small Christmas tree lay on its side, the decorations broken. He bent behind the chair she'd been sitting in and stood with a large rock in his hand. A white paper tied with twine was wound around it.

"What does it say?" Her voice shook. She watched as he removed the string and read it silently first, before meeting her eyes.

"Surrender the document or die."

She inhaled deep burning her lungs. "I dread the events of the future, not in themselves but in their results," she whispered.

"Quoting Edgar Allan Poe is not going to help you out of this one," he growled.

She glanced at him, curious at how he knew it was Mr. Poe she'd quoted but hadn't the time to pursue his intellect. She needed to get to Governor Black and now.

"I don't suppose you're going to tell me what document they speak of?" He reached for his cane and walked toward the window where he ran the end along the jagged glass clearing the frame of any sharp edges.

She watched him lean into the fancy walking stick and opened her mouth to confess when something struck her. Cole would be hunted, too. If she showed him the document they'd kill him and she couldn't live with that. He'd been her savior, even if he didn't know it, and when she glanced at him her heart warmed. Unsure what her feelings meant, she brushed them aside and gazed at him. Dark hair with the hint of grey at the temples fell around his face in unruly waves. The lines around his brown eyes showed the distress he'd been under, his lips held flat and unmoving and she wondered what he looked like when he smiled. *I cannot tell him.* Within the week she'd be dead if she didn't get the letter to the Governor.

"I'm sorry," she whispered and wrapped her good arm around herself to keep warm.

He gave her a glare cold enough to melt hell and went outside without his coat.

Cole's neighbor, Major Kindle, was standing outside when he slammed the front door behind him. Damn it. Why in hell won't she tell him what is going on?

"Colonel Black, I see you've had some trouble here," Kindle said staring at the broken window.

"I'm glad to see you're not blind, Major." He wasn't in the mood for chitchat. Someone wanted to kill his wife and—that was the second time today he'd referred to Matty as his wife. Might he be getting used to the idea of her company? No. He pushed aside any nostalgic feelings for the woman who deceived him and assessed the damaged window.

"No, not blind Colonel, but willing to help if you need it."

He sighed and his body gave a slight shiver against the blowing snow. He'd forgotten his coat and trudged back up the steps only to be met by Matty at the door holding the thick wool jacket. A blanket wrapped around her, she smiled and for the first time since he'd stepped outside he didn't feel the cold around him.

Cole hammered the last nail into the wood that covered the window, and bid Kindle farewell. He'd invited the Major and his wife for Christmas dinner. What the hell was the matter with him? He didn't entertain visitors, and he certainly didn't plan on being wed to Matty by then, either. Christmas Day they'd annul their marriage. A twinge of pain skipped across his chest, and he exhaled unwilling to imagine a life with Matty. He lived alone. He'd always be alone. He liked it that way.

He put most of his weight on his good leg and rotated the other one. The thigh cramped and he strained against the rolling torment as it surrounded the muscle and squeezed. He'd pushed the limb too far. His stomach turned, and he fought the nausea. He took small steps, pulling his leg behind him. Sweat beaded on his brow and dripped into his eyes, as his mouth watered with the urge to vomit. He reached for the doorknob when it swung open. Matty stood there, and reaching around his waist, she ushered him into the house.

"I'm fine," he said through clenched teeth.

"No you're not, but you will be soon." She helped him to his chair, propped his feet on the ottoman, and covered him with a blanket.

"Ice...I need ice for my leg." It was getting harder to speak as he battled with the bile lying dormant at the back of his throat. He would not vomit in front of her. He dug his fingers into the arm of the chair and flexed his jaw.

She left and returned with a bucket of snow. He watched through a haze as she wrapped a ball of ice into a dish towel and placed it gently on his thigh. He closed his eyes as the leg began to freeze and the pain subsided. A cool cloth was placed on his forehead while she smoothed back his hair. He started to doze when he felt her hesitant fingers fumble with the buttons on his coat. He removed the cloth from his forehead to stare at her.

Her bun was coming undone and blonde wisps clung to her temples. Rosy cheeks glowed against her pale face and he reached out his hand to run his thumb over the soft skin. She froze and her brown eyes gazed up at him. Fear, determination, and kindness were woven into the sable realms. She needed him for a reason he had yet to figure out. He'd never been needed before. He cupped his hand behind her head and brought her close. She bit the inside of her cheek to stop the trembling in her lips as her eyes questioned him. Cole brought his other hand to rest on her cheek as he bent toward her. He touched his lips to hers in a feathery kiss. He ran his tongue along her bottom lip when she moaned and leaned into him. The strangled cry had become the elixir he'd needed. Her hands moved to caress his neck and a dam burst within him, filling all the empty crevices to make him whole again.

He inhaled smelling smoke, when she froze and broke from his embrace.

"The stew is burning." She rushed from the room.

He leaned back into the chair content for the first time in years.

CHAPTER FIVE

"We are not going," Cole banged the end of his cane onto the floor.

"But it is on Christmas Eve and your father wants to see you," Matty tried not to beg. She'd handed him the letter after dinner not knowing what it contained. Now she knew nothing would stop her from seeing the Governor.

"Do you think it is wise to travel to Detroit while there is someone out there trying to kill you?"

"Danger knows full well that Caesar is more dangerous than he."

"Caesar is dead, damn it." He knocked his cane onto the hardwood.

"You will break it." She motioned to the cane.

"I have plenty in the closet."

"I am not afraid."

"The hell you aren't."

"I am not." She tipped her chin.

He stepped toward her. "Why are you hell bent on meeting Edward?"

"I merely want to see the Governor, that is all."

"Bull shit. You have another motive." He went to the mantel and poured himself a brandy. "I am not surprised. You are Delilah's kin."

She clenched her jaw at the insult. "I'd challenge you to a battle of wits but I see you are unarmed." The words were out before she could stop them.

"Love all, trust few, do wrong to none," he spat, his dark eyes cold.

The words slammed into her and she took a step back. *What am I doing?* "I apologise for my insolence."

He nodded.

"It is not in the stars to hold our destiny but in ourselves."

"Enough with the bloody quotes and talk like a damn human being!" he said as he slammed the end of his cane onto the hardwood. "Your destiny has death written all over it if you do not stay put."

If I stay I am doomed. He was determined to keep her here. She had to find a way to the Governor. After their kiss earlier, she witnessed a change in Cole. The hard lines on his face had softened before her eyes and his broad shoulders were no longer stiff and rigid. He'd been gentle, even kind toward her during dinner. She fancied the idea of staying married to him. Until truth sunk its sharp talons into her neck, reminding her that she'd deceived him and he'd want nothing to do with her after Christmas.

If I live until then.

She touched her lips. She'd watched the transformation within him when he caressed her. Unable to pull away, he'd captivated her into his embrace. When he touched his lips to hers, acceptance, hope, and a feeling of belonging filled her soul. If things were different—if she wasn't a maid who tricked him into marriage, would their paths have crossed? *Never.*

He pounded the cane twice onto the floor to get her attention. "Something is amiss. You're desperate to meet Edward, practically begging me to take you to him. Why?"

She opened her mouth to object when he held his hand up to stop her.

"General Worthington is who you are running from, isn't he?"

She swallowed loudly.

He stepped toward her and placed his hand on her arm. "Why does he want you dead?"

He was so close she could smell the brandy on his breath. She stepped away from him and placed her hands in the pocket of her apron to keep from touching him. She decided to try another tactic. "Please, I've never met a Governor."

He eyed her. "Begging will not change my mind nor will you changing the subject."

He didn't miss a thing. "I merely want to make his acquaintance, that is all." She averted her eyes. He'd been here when no one else had. He fought for her. She couldn't look at him for the guilt she felt.

"I find that hard to believe, Princess." He ran his hand through his hair only to have the long bangs fall back onto his face. "Why can't you trust me enough to tell me what you're running from?"

When she looked at him, all the lies she'd told crashed upon her shoulders and she reached for the mantel to keep steady. Her legs shook and she chewed her bottom lip. She owed him the truth. He'd proven his trust. *Confess.* She opened her mouth followed by silence. She tried again and still nothing. Her chest ached with the need to admit the truth, but her tongue would not cooperate. She blinked against the tears wanting to splash upon her cheeks and bowed her head.

"Matty, I can help you. Please, tell me why you need to see

Edward."

She witnessed the truth of his words in the two times he'd rescued her. A single tear fell onto her cheek. *He will die if I tell him.* "There are some secrets that do not permit themselves to be told," she whispered unwilling to come clean. *I am saving your life.*

"No there are not!" He slammed his cane across the edge of the fireplace sending the pine decorations onto the floor. The wood split into two and a folded white piece of paper floated above the fire.

"No!" She dived for the paper, catching it just before the flames licked it up.

Thank goodness, oh, thank goodness.

Cole snatched the letter from her hand before she could put it in her pocket.

"Please, Cole." She reached for the letter, but he held her away from him and scowled. "It is nothing but an old piece of paper."

"Your reaction tells me otherwise."

She flinched as he unfolded the letter she'd so carefully stuffed inside the hollow cane. *I am doomed.*

Cole read the letter four times before he could believe the words scribbled upon it. He glanced up at Matty. "This is treason."

She nodded.

The letter told of where the Union soldiers would attack next, giving the South the benefit and ability to ambush them.

"This is what you've been hiding from me all this time? This is why they want you dead."

"Yes."

"Where did you find it?"

"Three weeks ago I was dusting the General's office when I came upon it."

"You stole it?"

"Yes."

"Why would you put yourself in danger?"

"Innocent men are going to die. They're going to kill our soldiers."

"General Worthington, Major Smith and Captain Fillmore are among the names I'm familiar with, but there are others I do not know."

She bunched her apron in her hands squeezing the life from the fabric.

"Did you know the General was a part of this Secret Society?"

"Not until I'd read the letter." She sighed. "We need to take the document to your father. He is the only one who can help us."

He stared at the paper for a long time. The last person he wanted to see was Edward Black, but she was right, he had more pull when it came to this sort of thing. He'd issue military warrants for General

Worthington and the others. Even though Cole wished he could have that one pleasure. "We will leave in the morning."

Matty sat down by the fire and picked up a piece of the greenery she'd used to decorate the mantel. Her forehead no longer pulled tight from the burden she carried. Why did she think he wouldn't help her with something like this? It bothered him to think that she didn't trust him and wanted to make sure she knew he'd stand by her until this thing was finished.

He sat down in the chair beside her, the fire warming his legs. "Now, will you tell me everything?"

She nodded.

He folded up the document and placed it in his front pocket.

"I was able to elude the General for several days until he went into a rage demanding the paper from Eunice. He'd assumed it was her who took it, and he beat her so badly she lay in bed for two days. I knew then that I had to escape to save her. If I left he'd know I was the one who took the letter and Eunice would be safe. But I didn't have anywhere to go."

"Go on."

"I watched you when you'd come to dinner and I overheard that your father was the Governor. I figured you were my only chance at survival and getting the letter into safe hands. So I went to your house that night."

"I was drunk and you took advantage of the situation." He smirked.

"Not quite." She held her hands tight together and he resisted the urge to lay his palm over them and offer comfort. "I placed some laudanum in your drink."

"I knew it."

"But...but when I suggested we marry you agreed so quickly I thought I'd given you too much." She crossed her legs then uncrossed them while her fingers fiddled with the hem of her apron. He waited patiently for her to finish. "We...we never consummated, either. I lied to get you to stay married."

"So there is no baby?" He didn't know why he wasn't more relieved.

She shook her head, and with each tear that dripped from her lashes, he'd begun to understand how she must've felt.

"What's done cannot be undone, Princess." He wiped a tear away with the back of his hand.

"I will sign the annulment papers whenever you want." She looked into his eyes. "I am truly sorry, Cole."

"Let's straighten things out with this letter first and then we'll talk about the annulment."

She yawned and he guessed having held all this in for so long had taken its toll on her and she was exhausted.

"You need to get some rest."

"I am tired." She yawned again and her cheeks flushed pink.

"Good night then." He smiled.

She stood and walked to the bedroom door when she stopped and came back to stand in front of him. "Do not allow your ailment to shadow the man that you are. Without you, Cole I'd surely be dead by now. You are an asset to any situation and the military is lucky to have you." With those words she bent and brushed her lips across his whiskered cheek. "Goodnight and thank you."

He watched her go, a part of him wanting to follow her while the other fearful of what that meant. This past week somehow he'd taken to the idea of having a wife, something he'd never thought possible. Fighting alongside his men was all he'd ever wanted. He'd sent letter after letter only to have a few returned with denials. He must've done something wrong for the refusals but couldn't figure out what it was. He glanced at the bedroom door. Matty was different from all the other women he'd been introduced to. She didn't pity him for the way his life had changed, and other than the obvious reason she wanted to meet Edward Black, she never mentioned money or his stature as a Governor's son.

The boarded up window was a reminder to the danger they faced while traveling to Detroit tomorrow. He'd send for James and another soldier to escort them into the city. Christmas was in two days and that would give Cole and Edward enough time to plan things. He assumed General Worthington would attend the festivities along with a few others who were on the list. Cole ground his back teeth together and bunched his forearms. He'd love nothing more than to put his hands around the General's neck and watch the life fade from his beady eyes. He was a charlatan—a hypocrite who masqueraded as someone else. He relished in the ways of slavery, inflicting pain on those lower than him. Cole thought of Matty and how many beatings she must have taken under the hands of the Worthington's. Cole wanted to kill him.

CHAPTER SIX

Detroit, Michigan
Christmas Eve

Cole stood in his father's office waiting for Len Wiebe to arrive. He and Matty had gotten to Detroit late that morning and after escorting her to the hotel with strict instructions not to leave the room, he'd gone directly to Edward's home. After the governor had read the document he sent for Len, who ran the small Police department in Detroit.

"I must tell you, Coleman, I still cannot believe you are married," Edward said from behind his mahogany desk.

"It's Cole, and I am." He despised the man who sired him, but Matty was right, Edward was the only one who could put the warrants out. Nothing had changed between them in the last five years. Both men found it hard to be in the same room together and he struggled not to relive his childhood each time he saw the man who had abandoned him.

Edward had sent him to military school when he was nine years old, two days after the death of his mother. Alone and with no one to comfort him while he grieved, he'd placed all his anger into hating Edward. On his twelfth birthday he'd written to ask if he could come home and received no reply. When he graduated seven years later, Edward didn't bother to come. It wasn't until after he'd served his first mission in the army that he'd gone to see him. Edward had been cold and unwelcoming and Cole never returned, only seeing him through military events.

"Still hot headed I see." Edward pulled out a cigar and lit it filling the room with the musky scent.

"I am here for business and nothing more."

"Yes, so you've said." Edward inhaled a thick cloud of smoke. "It is awful that General Worthington has become caught up in this act of treachery. I never saw him as such."

"Some of us are good at disguising what we are," he growled.

"Boy, you need to let go of your anger. I did you a favor by placing you in that boarding school."

"Maybe, but I'll never thank you for it so stop thinking I will."

"Stubborn ass."

He turned away to stare out the window. The sky was a welcoming bright blue and the sun reflected off the snowy rooftops like sparkling diamonds. He thought of Matty and how she'd been cooped up indoors for over a week. Maybe he'd suggest a walk when he was done here.

"Sir, Mr. Wiebe is here," the butler announced.

"Send him in."

Cole turned from the window and leaned into his cane.

A tall lanky man burst through the doorway and he could tell from one glance he didn't like him.

"Governor Black, it is always nice to see you."

He was going to be sick. Len Wiebe was about as pretentious as Edward. No wonder the two got along.

"Len, this is my son, Colonel Black."

"Sir."

Cole nodded.

"I've called you here today because Colonel Black has brought it to my attention that a certain secret society is acting under the laws against treason." Edward took another pull from his cigar.

"What proof do you have of such a society?"

"This." Cole handed Len the document and waited while the man pulled out his spectacles to read it.

"What would you have me do?" Len asked the Governor.

"Why, arrest them of course," Edward said.

"But there are only three names on here that serve within Fort Wayne. We do not know the others."

"What you need to do, is place a warrant for the three men here. Edward will take care of the others by sending wires to the surrounding states and the Governors there," Cole interjected.

Len glanced at Edward.

"It will be done this afternoon," Edward said. "I have sent invitations to General Worthington, Major Smith and Captain Fillmore to attend my Christmas Eve dinner. You can arrest them when they arrive."

"Yes, Sir."

Cole didn't feel his presence was needed any longer. He'd wait until that evening to see the traitors arrested and behind bars.

"If you'll excuse me, I have other business to attend to," he said.

Both men nodded and he left, relieved to be out of the room and away from Edward. There was something in the way Len Wiebe looked at Edward that Cole didn't like. He was missing something, the hairs on the back of his neck told him so. On his way back to the hotel he went over the coming events when he passed a bookshop and stopped. For reasons he couldn't explain he went inside.

Matty stood in the foyer, her arm looped in Cole's as Edward Black greeted her with a kiss on the cheek.

"My lovely daughter-in-law, it is a pleasure."

The spicy cologne he wore tickled her nose and she forced down the sneeze that wanted to erupt. "Merry Christmas, Sir."

Cole pulled her along the wide hallway, introducing her to Senator Howard and his wife, General and Mrs. Gordon and her brother Captain Smith. She smiled and nodded as she was introduced to three more couples, all the while conscious that Colonel and Mrs. Worthington hadn't arrived yet.

Her stomach fluttered with waves of nausea and she slowed her steps. Cole escorted her into the sitting room where a large Christmas tree stood in front of the window. It was like nothing she'd ever seen before back home. Father had always insisted on having a tree even if it was no taller than his knee, and most years it was. She touched the red ribbon careful not to disturb the dried fruit sitting on the branch beside it.

"It is beautiful."

"Yes it is." He traced the ribbon with his finger.

"Major Smith and Captain Fillmore have been detained," Cole whispered into her ear.

"When?"

"They were arrested when they entered the city an hour ago."

"Why didn't you tell me?"

"I just found out from Senator Howard."

Cole looked handsome in his military uniform and she pulled her arm from his, needing some space. Tomorrow the traitorous men would be behind bars, Cole would annul their marriage, and she'd be left to find her way back home. If that was even possible; travel wasn't advised in some parts of the country due to the war. She couldn't stay at the Fort knowing he was there and so she'd take her chances.

Cole had found his way into her heart and she didn't know how to suppress her feelings for him any longer. She decided to keep her distance lest she make a fool of herself. Last night she allowed his arm to drape around her while he slept. Unprepared for the emotions that sprinkled over her, she buried her head into his arm, and released the tears allowing them to wash her soul. Helpless to the way he made her feel and powerless to do anything about it.

"Matty?"

She plastered a smile on her face and turned.

His brows furrowed and his dark eyes studied her. "You're flushed. Are you okay?"

She opened her mouth to thank him for being here when a

commotion in the other room drew them from the tree. The Senator stood in between General Worthington and Governor Black reading the document Matty had found. Three Policemen waited off to the side, hands held close to their pistols. Her insides turned, she straightened, trying to appear strong.

"This is absurd," General Worthington shouted. When he saw Matty his broad face turned a deep shade of red. "She has planted the letter to ruin me."

"You know that is not true," Cole said from beside her.

"She is nothing but a low-life serving girl. She cannot be trusted."

"She has been nothing but a thorn in our sides since we hired her," Mrs. Worthington added with her nose in the air.

She took a step back and was stopped by Cole's strong arm as it wrapped around her waist. She leaned into him unable to stand on her own.

"My wife has nothing to do with your decision to kill Union soldiers."

"Your wife will never be anything but a dirty house maid," General Worthington spat.

Cole stepped toward the General, when Edward put his arm up to stop him. "The evidence is in the letter."

"It states that the Union soldiers are heading to Fredericksburg, and where the Confederates can ambush them," Senator Howard said, disgust on his aged face.

"Take them away," Edward said.

"Sir, what of the missus?" the tallest of the three officers asked, and Matty turned toward him. There was something about him that was familiar.

He looked at her and she stared back unashamed of her boldness. *How do I know you?*

The corner of his mouth turned up, but his eyes remained cold.

"Take her, too," Edward said.

"Yes, Sir." He winked at Matty before he left with Mrs. Worthington.

He was one of them. She tightened every muscle in her body and left Cole's arms to go into the other room.

Cole followed.

"Did you know the policeman who took Mrs. Worthington?" she asked.

"No, I am not familiar with who Edward hires to run the city."

His father hired the policemen? This cannot be. She was sure the Officer was one of the men who had tried to kill her the day they were ambushed. She glanced at him. *How do I tell him and what if I am wrong?* Of all the guests in the room, he was the only one she trusted.

"I think he was one of the men who ambushed us," she whispered.

"Are you sure?"

She nodded. "It was his voice. The way it went up and down. I remembered it. The Officer had the same voice."

"There are a lot of people who speak the same way, Matty. We cannot assume he is the one. I'm positive General Worthington sent them with the other soldiers to Fredericksburg."

Disappointment turned her eyes down and she shrugged. "Maybe you're right." But she knew better. Her back rigid, she followed Cole into the dining room, watchful of those around her.

Edward Black's kitchen staff put on a wonderful meal of roasted duck, potatoes, carrots and dessert, but she had no appetite. She couldn't help the unsettling feeling that things weren't what they seemed here. She glanced at Cole while he took a bite of his pie, and wondered why he hadn't picked up on it.

She excused herself to use the facilities but to also have a look around. If Governor Black hired the policemen then he'd be a part of the Secret Society trying to kill Union soldiers. *Let no such man be trusted.* She opened a large oak door. The hinges creaked and she stopped to see if anyone came to investigate the noise. She stepped inside the Governor's office and rushed to the mahogany desk.

Matty searched the papers on top of the large desk careful not to disturb their place. When she found nothing there she opened the top drawer and rustled through the documents. *Nothing. Maybe I am wrong.* She struggled to open the bottom drawer, and was shocked when there were only a few papers within it. *Why was it so heavy?* She pulled out the papers and saw the small handle on the bottom of the drawer.

Cautious not to make a sound, she quietly pulled the wooden board out laying it on the floor beside her. Documents stamped with the president's seal stood before her. She pulled them out when something fell from the stack to land on the floor and roll under the desk. On her hands and knees she grabbed it.

Shock stole the breath from her lungs and kicked her heart into spasms. *Why would he have this?* Eyes wide, she stared at the heavy marker bearing the President's seal. She glanced at the papers she let fall from her lap and spotted Cole's signature. It was his appeal. She rummaged through more and found four others he'd written. *Edward Black was denying his own son's petitions to fight in the war by disguising himself as the President.* But why?

"May I help you, daughter?" Edward asked.

"Double double, toil and trouble; fire burn and cauldron bubble." She stood holding the marker and letters Cole had written.

"You are in a lot of trouble." He advanced and she stepped back tripping over the opened drawer. He landed on top of her and was quick to wrap his hands around her neck. "No one needs to see those letters."

She struggled against his grip, kicking her legs while she thrashed beneath him. He was too heavy for her to move. She gasped, desperate to scream for Cole. Black dots danced in front of her and she blinked trying to focus. She had to stay awake. She needed air!

Edward laughed above her as his hands tightened on her throat…he was going to kill her.

Cole. The room blurred and she blinked frantic to live. *Cole.* She didn't feel her arms as they fell from Edward's shoulders to the floor. She pushed out her tongue trying to form a word. *Cole.*

Edward was thrown from her, the pressure on her neck gone, and she sucked in a cleansing breath. She rolled over coughing and wheezing as the cold air pushed into her lungs. She heard Cole's curse rub against the one Edward shot back. The large bookshelf fell from the wall as they smashed into it. She crawled toward the window and pulled herself upright, the letters still clenched in her hands.

The Senator and two other men burst into the room and pulled them apart. Father and son glared at each other, while their chests heaved.

"What in bloody blazes is going on?" Senator Howard yelled.

"He tried to kill my wife," Cole said while wiping blood from the cut on his lip.

"Is this true?" the Senator asked.

"Yes, it is. But I had my reasons. She is the traitor. I found her rummaging through my desk. I believe her to be the Napoleon in this whole treasonous mess."

The three women standing in the hall gasped.

"You're a damn liar," Cole yelled.

Matty tried to find her voice, but all she could do was whisper. She waved Cole over, ignoring the apology in his eyes and handed him the papers.

He leaned toward her. "What are these?"

"I found them hidden in your father's desk," she squeaked.

The room was quiet as Cole read the letters. "You rotten son of a bitch." He went for Edward but was stopped by General Gordon and Captain Smith.

"What is it, boy?" the Senator asked.

"Edward Black forged the President's seal."

The room erupted as everyone talked at once.

"I've done no such thing!" Edward yelled and she saw him kick the seal under the chair beside him.

She stomped her foot to get Cole's attention and pointed to the chair.

Cole slid the plush furniture to the side and picked up the fake seal.

"I love my son. I didn't want him to be killed," Edward whined.

"You will hang for this," Senator Howard growled.

"Why would you do this?" Cole asked. "What reason do you have for keeping me out of battle?"

"Like I said, I don't want to see you hurt." Edward hunched his back and pulled his features down into a sad face. "Coleman, you've been shot and almost killed once. I couldn't bear to lose you."

"Bull shit. There has never been any love between us. There is another reason you don't want me out there."

Matty pushed against the wall and stood. She went to Cole and handed him another letter. He placed his arm around her waist and she leaned against him while he read it.

"I should've known, you traitorous bastard." Cole motioned for the Senator and handed the man the letter. "You're one of them."

"Detain him," he said to General Gordon.

More furniture was pushed out of the way as the men went for Edward. Cole escorted Matty from the room to the front door where James stood outside. He winced as he shifted onto his good leg and she stopped, waiting for him to get his balance. He set his jaw as he grabbed her coat from the butler. Strong arms encircled her and she wanted nothing more than to lean into them, but instead pushed her shoulders forward.

"Take her to the hotel." He passed Matty to James. "I'll follow once things are settled here."

"Yes, sir."

The cold air assaulted her causing her teeth to chatter. She pulled her coat tighter and tipped her chin against the blowing wind. The weather didn't seem to bother James as he walked alongside her. She glanced behind her at the door where Cole stood watching them. Her chest constricted as the reality of what she was losing ripped at her soul. Helpless to what the future held, she turned from him and walked back to the hotel.

CHAPTER SEVEN

December 25th

Matty woke to the first rays of sun shining through the hotel window. Cole hadn't come back last night and she'd fallen asleep in her gown waiting for him to arrive. She sighed and ignored the loneliness as it settled around her heart. She clamped her lips together reluctant to surrender to her own feelings.

She removed her dress, replacing it with the brown, plain one she always wore. She stood and looked out the window. Thick white flakes fell from the grey sky and she searched the streets for any sign of Cole. The dull ache wrapped around her spine and she gasped. A sob lay at the back of her throat and she crossed her arms for comfort. Today she'd annul her marriage and leave Cole behind—deserting the only person who she felt safe with.

The door opened and Cole entered the room. He leaned into his cane, his uniform wrinkled and his hair hanging in loose curls around his tired eyes.

"Your leg—

"It's fine."

"Where have you been?" she asked. It was too difficult to look at him so she focused on the wall behind him instead.

"I needed to wait with the Senator for the soldiers to arrive from the Fort to guard the prisoners."

"What will happen to them?"

"Most likely, they'll hang."

"I'm sorry Cole. I never meant for this to happen."

"Edward made his decisions and he will have to face the consequences."

"Years of love have been forgot, in the hatred of a minute."

"There was never any love. I didn't know him." He stared at her brown bag beside the chair. "Have you packed?"

"Yes, I thought you'd want to get things cleared up between us."
He nodded. "I will change and we can head on down."

The city was quiet and she'd almost forgotten that it was Christmas morning. The stores were closed, the owners at home with their families. She should be celebrating her newfound freedom. Thanks to Cole she no longer had to be afraid that someone wanted her dead. She peered at him through her lashes. Haggard and worn, he was still as handsome as the first time she'd seen him.

Why couldn't things be different between them? She battled with whether to cry or scream and instead tried to concentrate on placing one foot in front of the other while they walked. The snow crunched with each step they took and she licked a snowflake from her lips.

She wasn't familiar with Detroit and followed him to Senator Howard's residence. According to Cole, a judge wouldn't be passing through for another week, so the Senator was their only choice for an annulment.

It was clear he no longer wanted any association with her and she couldn't blame him. He'd been nothing but honest about living his life alone and she had to accept that. He came from wealth and she from dirt. Society didn't put them on the same shelf. It was that simple.

"How far is Senator Howard's home?"

"Two blocks south of here."

"I see."

"I'd like to show you something first, if you don't mind." He took her hand in his and pulled her off the main street and onto a path behind Donnelly's General store.

She dug her heals in. "I'm not too sure—"

He ignored her, tugging on her arm as they walked. The path narrowed and Cole stepped in front of her. She could no longer see where they were going, and when he stopped suddenly she ran into his back. He pushed the cane into the snow to catch his balance and she murmured an apology.

A weathered building stood in front of them. Cole took a key out of his pocket and opened the door. When he brought her inside she stopped. The smell of paper teased her nostrils and she couldn't help the smile as it spread across her face. As a young girl the smell of a book always brightened her day.

He lit a lantern and she stared in awe at the tall shelves before her, littered with books.

"Where are we?"

He turned and faced her. "The bookstore."

She touched the blue binding to her left and read the name, Moby

Dick by Herman Melville. "I've heard of this book, but had never thought to read it."

"You can pick three."

"Excuse me?"

He smiled and her insides warmed.

"I've arranged for you to pick three books at my expense."

She bristled. "I do not need your pity."

"It's not pity."

"Poor and content is rich and rich enough."

He laughed.

"Quote whatever you like, Princess. But it isn't pity I feel for you."

She gave him a scathing glare. "Then what is it?"

His dark eyes softened, and he reached for her hand. "Love."

Her eyes misted. "Love?"

"I've never been in love, Matty." He wiped a tear from her cheek. "But I cannot see past today without you in it."

"Cole."

He opened her palm and placed a heart shaped locket within it. "I give you my heart if you'll have it." He brought his lips to hers and whispered, "Doubt the stars are fire, doubt that the sun doth move; doubt truth to be a liar—"

"But never doubt thy love," she finished bringing her lips to his.

~ * ~

If you enjoyed this book, please consider writing a short review and posting it on Amazon, Goodreads and/or Barnes and Noble. Reviews are very helpful to other readers and are greatly appreciated by authors, especially me. When you post a review, drop me an email and let me know and I may feature part of it on my blog/site. Thank you. ~ Kat

katflannery@shaw.ca

From the Authors

Dear Reader,

Writing a feel-good romance set in the American Civil War was a bit of a challenge. More Americans died in the Civil War than in World War I, World War II, the Korean War and the Vietnam War combined. Then there was the institutionalized inhumanity of slavery. Still, no matter what the circumstances, people can rise above adversity.

Maggie and Matty rise. Separated from their family, they create new ones. They face their fears and find humor and romance, as so many people have in the past, even in the darkest moments

Cheers – Alison and Kat

About the Authors

Alison Bruce

Alison Bruce has an honors degree in history and philosophy, which has nothing to do with any regular job she's held since. A liberal arts education did prepare her to be a writer, however. She penned her first novel during lectures while pretending to take notes.

In addition to being the author of mystery, romantic suspense and historical romance novels, Alison has had many careers. Copywriter and editor since 1992, she has also been a comic book store manager, small press publisher, web designer and arithmetically challenged bookkeeper.

Her current careers include Publication Manager of Crime Writers of Canada, Arthur Ellis Awards Administrator and part-time tech guru to the technologically challenged.

Website: http://www.alisonbruce.ca

Blog: http://alisonebruce.blogspot.ca

Twitter: https://twitter.com/alisonebruce

Facebook: https://www.facebook.com/alisonbruce.books

Kat Flannery

Kat Flannery's love of history shows in her novels. She is an avid reader of historical, suspense, paranormal, and romance.

When not researching for her next book, Kat can be found running her three sons to hockey and lacrosse.

She has her Certificate in Freelance and Business Writing. A member of many writing groups,

Kat enjoys promoting other authors on her blog. She's been published in numerous periodicals.

This is Kat's third book and she is hard at work on her next.

Website: www.katflannery-author.com

Blog: www.kat-scratch.blogspot.ca

Twitter: https://twitter.com/katflannery1

Facebook:
http://www.facebook.com/pages/Kat-Flannery/131065966999142

IMAJIN BOOKS

Quality fiction beyond your wildest dreams

For your next eBook or paperback purchase, please visit:

www.imajinbooks.com

www.twitter.com/imajinbooks

www.facebook.com/imajinbooks

Made in the USA
Charleston, SC
28 September 2013